Ice Island

Morgan's Knot – A Serial Fantasy

Episode III

By

Eric T. Stiller, Jr.

For Wee Henry

Ice Island

Morgan's Knot – A Serial Fantasy
Episode III

Adrian stood alone on the bow of the Jasmine as it plowed through deep swells in the North Atlantic. Sunlight shimmered across surging whitecaps spewing froth on a frigid northerly gale and seagulls swooped and soared hopefully around the stern of the hardy fishing boat. A squadron of pelicans, coasting in graceful formation, crossed their bow a few feet above the waves searching for a school of fish near the surface.

The old trawler was crammed to overflowing with the original crew and his parents, as well as Sammy and Simian, who joined the voyage in Jamaica. He wondered whether George had already returned to Morgan's Knot from the Island of the Children. He loved them all but this was the only place on the ship where he could be alone with his thoughts.

He leaned out to gaze down the sturdy curve of the bow slicing through the sea. The two dolphins, Spot and Dusty, were playing tag and guiding them home through icy black waters. They were close to Morgan's Knot and he wanted to watch it rise out of the horizon.

The last time he approached the island on his parents' sloop, the Sparrow, he was a homesick boy on his way to visit his aunt and uncle for the summer. So much had happened in the past months and he felt that the lessons learned were merely preparation for the next twist along a path that was relentlessly drawing him into this strange and mysterious culture. The ordinary boy daydreaming about summer adventures, as he awaited the final seconds of the last day of school at the Heritage Academy, seemed an innocent apparition from another lifetime.

He flashed on the battle on the mountain, rescuing Ester, the journey to find his parents, and panicked pirates fleeing the Island of the Children. Raffe's enthusiasm, as they viewed the history of the descendants of Protus inscribed on the chamber within the pyramid, proved that there could be other allies around the world. The new *seer* wanted to learn everything there was to know about the history of his ancestors, the powers of the Crystals, and secrets yet to be discovered in the Book of Natural Balance. And then he found Sammy and Simian.

In reflection, it seemed that Adrian's experience with the Books and the Crystals was confined to solving mysteries, overcoming obstacles, and finding the means of saving their way of life. He wondered whether there was more depth in the Books chronicling the ancients who first ignited the torch to defend all that is right and true. As Raffe pointed out, they contained the history of his ancestors and all those who struggled to maintain The Balance but he had yet to find insightful references to those who mastered the Black Crystals and there was the most intriguing question of whether the Books could predict the future. There was so much that he wanted to learn and he looked forward to spending time in Ponte's observatory, studying the texts with his friend, Alius. He missed her on this journey and wondered what she learned in his absence.

A screech from Magnus, circling several hundred feet above the old trawler, roused him from Spot and Dusty to scan the horizon to the north where a dark lump was beginning to rise from the sea. He turned to yell, "Land Ho!"

Suddenly, everyone on the boat was moving to find a spot where they could see the island and an anxious air of anticipation broke into smiles and cheers, as they closed on Morgan's Knot.

Morgan wandered over to Adrian and draped a long arm around his shoulders. He looked up into her beautiful eyes. "You seem a bit withdrawn," she said quietly. "I've been worried about you."

"It's nothing," replied Adrian shyly. "I guess I've been feeling kind of squashed with all the people on the boat. I needed to find a place to be alone for a while, just to have a chance to think about all that we've been through in the past few months."

"I know how you feel," whispered Morgan, tilting her head slightly forward. "Am I interrupting?"

"Oh, no," smiled Adrian, as he put his arm around her waist. It still annoyed him that she was taller and more mature but she was genuinely kind and caring…and smart. She looked beautiful with her hair flowing in the wind, her skin tanned by the tropical sun, and those gorgeous green eyes. "It's not you or anyone in particular, for that matter. I just feel…restless."

"Me too, it's been a long voyage." Morgan hugged him gently, "It'll be good to be on dry land at home."

"It's funny, but after these few months, Morgan's Knot is home. When I arrived on the island, all I could think about was how to make the time go faster, so I could join my parents in Vancouver." He paused, gazing across the black water to the island. "That seems a very long time ago."

"I think that everyone on the island is grateful for all you've done and we're all proud of the person you've become."

Adrian blushed, "I only did what I had to do."

"Most of us wouldn't have known what to do, let alone found the courage to try some of the things you've tackled."

"I almost wish that everyone didn't know," sighed Adrian, as he watched Magnus circling ahead of the old trawler.

"The first time I met you on the beach, I thought you were kind of shy," said Morgan quietly. "But there isn't one person, North or South, on Morgan's Knot and, now on The Island of the Children, who isn't thankful that you stepped up at the critical moment. You're a celebrity."

"I know but that position includes an expectation of the person they want me to be. Sometimes, I wonder whether I really am that person." Tears welled in his eyes.

Morgan pulled him close, with a gentle smile graced in sincere kindness, and wiped the tears from his cheeks with her thumb. "Listen to me. You're a boy who's been asked to do things that grown men would hesitate to try. You've been pushed beyond your years and still managed to save a way of life for hundreds, no - thousands of people." She kissed him on the forehead, "Perhaps, you just need some time to be a boy again."

"Maybe."

"You can't go back to being the person you were when you arrived on the island and you can't stop being famous for the things that you've done. All you can do is be the best you can be. Everything else will fall into place."

"To tell you the truth, I'm kind of looking forward to going back to school, taking classes, and having some time to play."

"I know how you feel," smiled Morgan. "If you need someone to talk with about all of this, I'll be happy to listen."

"Thanks," said Adrian quietly, with a hug.

Everyone hustled around the trawler, stowing gear and packing the last of their things, as Kelly idled the ship around the point into the entrance to the harbor. It would be good to be home.

Chapter 2

The last of the representatives scurried along the dank tunnel and filed into an enormous theater carved out of dense volcanic stone beneath the desolate island. Transported on small, silent submarines that surfaced and docked in an underground cavern, they had no geographical key to their destination. The satellite recognizance of the superpowers could not see the thriving city that had been spawned under the ice-covered rock in the middle of the ocean and its isolated location, far removed from shipping lanes, guaranteed secrecy.

The audience was comprised of men from every corner of the globe. Each had attained positions of power within their political, economic, and religious institutions, yet they remained in the shadows, out of sight from the press or the intelligence services. Throughout history, there have been rumors of a secret society guiding events throughout the world, promoting and electing the leaders of the major countries and religions, manipulating the global economy, and profiting from fabricated conflicts.

An elite clique controlled the media to quash those fables and those powers were well represented in this assembly. This exclusive group of one hundred was known in the Legion of Darkness as 'The Whisperers'.

Behind a small platform, a giant Black Crystal rotated several feet above the floor. Illuminated by colored *orbs* concealed in the ceiling and walls, the enormous gem traced dazzling blue-black glimmers around the darkened room. A commanding voice reverberated from loudspeakers surrounding the audience, "Distinguished friends and honored guests, it is my distinct honor and privilege to introduce Lord Zepallo, representing the Council of Ollapez."

A spotlight flashed from the domed ceiling, focused on a small dais in front of the Crystal. Out of thin air, a tall slender figure shrouded in black robes materialized. A pale gaunt face framed intense blue eyes staring from beneath a cowl at the crowd of captivated faces peering back through the darkness. The members of the audience stood to applaud, bowing out of respect or fear or both.

A deep resonant voice filled the room, as be bowed, "Legio Obscurum!"

The Whisperers raised their fists in a salute of allegiance.

He paused as they took their seats, gazing around at the eyes of some of the most powerful men in the world, glistening and focused in rapt anticipation. "My friends, we are gathered here to celebrate our successes and to plan for the future domination of the world. Our forefathers attempted…and failed…to use the vast energies of the Black Powers to annihilate our enemies. The history books are filled with examples of their disastrous and misguided campaigns."

"Our technicians are combining the energies of the vectors from all of the Dark Crystals into a vast web surrounding the globe and, when their work is completed, we will control the ultimate power on the planet!"

Cheers and applause.

"As the events of the past few months demonstrate, our influence is coalescing. We are witnessing the birth of a global conflict between North and South, East and West, between the religions of the East and those born of the Holy Land, between the haves and have-nots, between all races, societies, tribes, and countries."

"We'll not raise our swords, as we have no need to sacrifice a single warrior to armed conflict, for those who have gathered here can and will lead their institutions into a Third World War! We will force the fools, so carefully placed in leadership positions in the most powerful countries in the world, to fight our battles for us." He paused to scan a captivated audience, his voice rising from a haunting whisper to a crescendo, "We will rise from the ashes of world conflict as the voice of reason and stability and you will lead the entire population of the planet to a new order…a dark order!"

The Whisperers jumped to their feet.

Lord Zepallo raised pale slender hands for silence, "Each of you will receive new directives and we trust that you will follow them precisely. The future of the world, our world, depends on absolute obedience and meticulous execution of our plans. I have faith in your abilities and your dedication to the path that we must follow. The next phase of this global disruption has already begun and, with your vigilance, we will succeed!"

Again, the audience rose to clap and cheer. Lord Zepallo raised his hands, as if blessing his emissaries to go forth and destroy the foundations of civilization. With a sinister smirk, he lowered his head and dissolved into the darkness of the room. The applause continued for several moments after the lights came up and the spotlight dimmed on the empty dais.

Dark-robed attendants moved through the crowd, delivering scrolls to each of the members of the audience. The voice from the speakers instructed, "You will commit these documents to memory and return them to the attendants waiting at each exit. All of the scrolls must be collected before you leave this room."

The audience was silent for nearly half an hour, as each absorbed their orders from the documents. There were occasional gasps and murmurs, as the commands were digested and memorized. No one spoke.

As each envoy finished, they rose and moved to the exits. The scrolls were returned to the sentries, along with large black diamonds that had been suspended around their necks as protection from the immense powers of the Black Crystal, and the group slowly shuffled into the passageways surrounding the conference chamber.

The Reverend Crosby whispered to the High-Lord Barrett, "Who is Lord Zepallo and how has he suddenly become the voice of the Council?"

The High-Lord leaned to murmur, "It is said that he was born in Jerusalem and served for a time in the Vatican, but, beyond that, I honestly don't have an answer to your question. Ten years ago, he took a seat on the Council without explanation or open support from any wing of our political spectrum. They say his influence dominates the aging Council and there are rumors that he's positioned himself in direct line for the throne but, in the process, he has amassed an immense fortune and, quietly and subtly, controls many of the world's largest corporations from behind the scenes. No one knows where he actually lives or how he moves about the world. He just appears, as he did this evening, and then disappears. He is a living ghost but I have no doubt that everything we heard tonight is true. As frightening as it might be, I trust that his plan for the salvation of the world, our world, will come to pass as he has predicted."

"We have our orders and we shall see it through to the end. We must succeed and we will."

Chapter 3

An anxious crowd of several hundred lined the docks as the Jasmine rounded the jetties. A raucous cheer went up as lines were tossed from the trawler, while Kelly gently revved the engines in reverse to settle the ship against the dock and leaned out the window with a radiant smile. The children scrambled into the waiting arms of their parents and Adrian spied Elsie and George, who were standing with Ester, Nanchez, Mandor, Jofre, and Alius.

John helped Sara onto the dock and into her sister's embrace. Adrian hopped onto the wharf to hug Alius, "I'm so glad to see you!"

"I'm just happy you made it back safely. I've missed you. Everyone is so proud of all of you and I can't wait to hear your story!"

"We'll have time for that. I'm looking forward to getting back to work on The Books with you."

"Believe me, I can use the help. Nanchez and Ester have been keeping me busy."

Adrian turned to his uncle, "When did you get back?"

George smiled, "Last night. I'm still confused about what time it is…I think I'm still on La Isle de Los Ninas time."

"I'm kind of jealous that your journey was way faster than ours. Did you finish with all you were trying to accomplish?"

"Pretty much," smiled his uncle, lifting his weathered hat to smooth back his gray hair. "The first fields are planted, their accounts are set up on the mainland, and we found suppliers who can provide almost everything they need. In fact, we even found a quarry with stone that matches the stone in the old city. They've already started demolition."

"I miss them but it sure is nice to be back on Morgan's Knot!"

Ponte emerged from Ester's embrace and turned to introduce Simian and Sammy to Nanchez, Mandor and Jofre. Adrian noticed the giant Keeper lean to whisper in Ponte's ear. The Professor's smile deflated into a concerned scowl, as the two men wandered away from the crowd in quiet consultation, and Adrian wondered what they were discussing. *"I guess we'll find out soon enough,"* he thought.

He turned close to Alius and asked, quietly, "Is there something I should know?"

"There's some technical mystery but I haven't figured it out yet. Nanchez has been asking questions about the power of the Black Crystal and the vector system," replied Alius. "That's one of the reasons that I'm so glad you're back. Maybe we can figure out what he's so anxious about. He's been downright cranky."

Adrian turned as Nanchez' truck roared up through the little village in a cloud of dust with Simian and Sammy in the back, holding Tic and smiling broadly as they crested the hill and turned north to the observatory.

Sara, John, Elsie and George led a procession back to the House of the Four Seasons in the trolley and Molly drove Alius, Megan, and Adrian back in the wagon.

Adrian gazed around the island as they rolled along tree-lined paths through fields lush and green. There was no evidence of the damage from the storm, almost as if he was remembering a childish nightmare from another lifetime.

He shivered as he looked north to the mountain, noticing a thin trail snaking up the black rock to allow vehicles to pass back and forth from North and South. A few months had passed since he and Alius battled at the Knot and the new road was a symbol of the concessions made by the adults on both sides. Turning to Alius, he said, "It looks like everyone's been busy!"

"A lot has changed for the better. Former aliens are melding with each other and the technologies, of the North and South, are being merged. At times, it almost seems as if the walls that separated the two sides never existed."

"I'm sorry I wasn't here to help."

"I've learned a lot while you were gone but I'm happy you're back. I have a feeling that Ponte and Nanchez are going to pester us. Besides, school starts next week and I can't wait to take Ponte's astronomy class!"

"Me too! I have a feeling that he'll be adding several other courses. We've learned a lot but our magic pales in comparison with what they've developed on the Island of the Children. I can't wait to teach you about flying through the water!"

"I don't understand," smiled Alius.

"We've brought back some very special diving suits that allow you to move through the water at high speeds. The feeling is exhilarating and the life that exists under the surface of the ocean is amazing. They have an entire city under the sea!"

"If we hadn't been communicating with Dadeus and Gabrielle, I'd think you were kidding!" Alius' blue eyes sparkled.

Adrian felt a familiar bump as they passed through the gate and noticed the garden overflowing with growth. Everything was an intense green that made the colors of the fruits, flowers, and vegetables almost electric. His first view of the old house reminded him of the first evening he arrived with his parents, only months ago.

Molly pulled to a stop behind the trolley at the front door and they all piled out, gathered their bags, and hiked up the front steps. Adrian paused to pat the small plaque next to the front door 'The House of the Four Seasons'. *It's good to be home.*"

The children grabbed *orbs* from the carrier and trouped up the stairs. As they reached the second floor, Sara asked, "May I borrow your key?"

Adrian smiled, pulling the golden key from his pocket and handing it to his mother. She inserted it into the lock of a door at the far end of the hall from Adrian's room. A deep voice asked, "Who seeks entry?"

"I am Sara," grinned his mother, surprising an old friend.

"Ah, Sara. It is nice to have you home!" The door swung open and Sara returned the key to Adrian with a grin and a kiss on the forehead, as his father carried their small bags into the room. Besides the robes that everyone wore on the Island of the Children, they had purchased a few pieces of clothing while they were in Jamaica and Simian had given his mother a large piece of the beautiful blue fabric from his stall. The rest of their clothes were lost in the shipwreck or packed in boxes in Vancouver.

As Adrian turned down the hall, his door swung open, "I've been wondering when you would return!"

"I'm back and I hope to be staying for a while," replied Adrian, as the lamps sprang to life and flames leapt from the few logs in the tiny fireplace. Alius followed him into the room.

"It's so nice to be here," said Adrian, as he laid his bags and the *orb* on his bed.

"We've all missed you," said Alius. "There's so much I want to tell you and even more I want to hear about."

Adrian opened a small bag and pulled out his robes and then his diving gear. "This is the suit that I was telling you about. It has a breathing device and communications in the headpiece. When you enter the water, a bubble of air forms that makes your body slippery enough to speed through the sea. My mother spent a lot of time with the tailors on the Island of the Children learning how to construct these suits and she's hoping they can make them for everyone on the island. We've only been using part of the powers of the Crystal!"

Molly and Megan, dressed in their diving suits, peeked in the door. Adrian and Alius doubled over in laughter, as the two girls did a little soft-shoe shuffle framed at the threshold.

Molly's muffled voice cried out, "I can't wait to try these out on our favorite beach with Spot and Dusty!"

Megan moaned, "These are hot when you're out of the water, I've gotta take this off!"

Adrian and Alius settled on the floor, still giggling at the antics of the girls. "I've met more *seers*. Two on the Island...a lady, named Mary, and a boy, Raffe, who's about our age. We think Simian and, perhaps Sammy, are also *seers* but we'll test them."

"I was wondering where you found them and why they came back with you."

"That's a long story but, for the moment, they live in Montego Bay. Simian has this weird ability to travel along the vectors by what seems sheer willpower. One moment, we were in his fabric stall in the market and, the next thing I knew, we were miles away, standing in a cavern where their Green Crystal is hidden. Somehow, he can see what's happening along the vectors. I've promised to teach him about the Book of Wisdoms in exchange for learning about his amazing talent."

"You're joking!" laughed Alius.

"You know me better than that. I don't joke about the powers," replied Adrian with a grin.

"You're serious," said Alius. "If what you're saying is true, then I want to learn everything that I can from them!"

"I've been thinking about all of that. The trip back seemed to take twice as long as our journey to the Pacific and I've had a lot of time to think about our talents, The Books, and The Crystals."

"The first thing I realized was that we're not alone, there are other *seers* and Keepers out there working with other Crystals. After seeing the wonders the people of the underworld have created around their Ruby Crystal, then realizing that there was a Crystal in Jamaica and that Simian was probably an untrained *seer* who understands lots of things that we don't know, it just seemed to open up the possibilities. I really feel that we're a very small part of something much bigger."

"I know what you mean," said Alius. "I keep feeling that there are layers and layers of information in the Book of Knowledge and the

Book of Wisdoms. It almost seems like an onion, you peel away one layer and find another and then another."

"My friend, Raffe, didn't know he was a *seer*…just as I didn't know," said Adrian, smiling as he pondered the thought. "His first reaction was that he wanted to know everything about his ancestors, about the people who discovered all of this and those who carried this knowledge through thousands of years. That led me to wonder whether the Books contain not only our history but our future?"

Alius was quiet for a moment as she thought about his inspiration, "I see what you mean. We've been asked to answer technical questions and we've only seen one small part of something that seems much larger. When I was alone with the Silver Book, I used to ask stupid questions, like whether I'd ever get a chance to get off this island or whether I'd get married someday. I didn't know enough to ask important questions but I always felt like I was dipping my pinky finger into the ocean."

"Right, it's knowing what to ask isn't it? The other question that I came up with was whether there are *seers* working with the Black Crystals, only on a bigger scale than you did before I convinced you to see the Balance."

Alius burst out laughing and raised her fists, "Do you want to go another round with me? I'll whip your butt this time!"

Adrian rolled around on the floor laughing. It was good to be home with his favorite *seer*.

The girls popped back into Adrian's room. Megan said, "We need to go outside and, besides, Mom wants us to pick some veggies for dinner."

"I won't even complain," said Adrian. "It will be so good to have a dinner from the garden!"

The children trouped down the stairs, deposited their *orbs* in the carrier, grabbed a couple of baskets in the kitchen, and headed out the south door into the sunshine.

Bessie, the mule, and a couple of goats wandered over from the barn, "Welcome home!"

The children hugged the animals and Megan said, "It's so nice to be home and to see all of you. We've missed your magic!"

Several sheep, a pony, a couple of pigs, chickens, ducks, and a few geese joined the revelry, songbirds flew around their heads, and the herd wandered over to the garden to collect the vegetables for dinner.

Chapter 4

Adrian awoke to his mother's kiss on his cheek. He yawned, rubbed his eyes, and smiled up at her.

"Ponte's on the *messenger*. He wants to talk with you," she said quietly.

He rolled out of bed and padded after his mother down the stairs to George's study. Ponte's face glowed on the *messenger*. He looked tired and impatient.

"Good morning, Professor," said Adrian, yawning.

"Good morning, my boy," said Ponte hurriedly, "I was wondering whether you might come by the observatory this morning, I could use your assistance. I've already called Alius and she'll be here within the hour."

"I'd be happy to help," said Adrian, "I'll be there as soon as I can."

"Right, then," muttered Ponte, already turning away from the *messenger* as his image disappeared.

"I wonder what that was about?"

"He certainly didn't seem himself," said Sara. "One of us can drive you up there after breakfast. Why don't you go get dressed and I'll fix you something to eat."

"Okay," said Adrian turning back to the stairs. *"Alius said that Nanchez was having a problem with the Black Crystal. I guess I'm about to find out what's going on."*

Ester opened the door before Adrian reached the stoop. "It's lovely to have you back!" she said, wrapping a long boney arm around his shoulders.

"It's nice to be home," replied Adrian with a smile.

"Come in, come in." She ran her hand through his mop of blond hair, "All of you are so tan and you could use a haircut!"

"Well, I was kind of busy but my mother's going to cut it in the next day or two," he smiled.

Adrian walked into the parlor and stopped at the couch to pet Tic, who rolled over on his back to stretch. "I'm glad to see that you found your favorite spot!"

"I'll go outside, as soon as it warms up, but it sure is nice to be napping without worrying about looking after you," smiled Tic.

Adrian laughed, "Touché!" He gazed around the room, its walls lined with thousands of books and strange objects. He had forgotten the wonder of the moving star map that glowed in the ceiling and the model of the solar system hanging in mid-air, colored *orbs* - the planets and tiny moons - orbiting a glowing sun at the center. Cases of electronic equipment overflowed in a tangle of wires, switches, dials, and gauges and he noticed that the cages, once occupied by the hawks, Magnus, and the snakes, stood empty. The three-dimensional chess set sat above the table in front of the sofa. The arrangement of the pieces inside the grid suggested a game patiently awaiting completion.

He walked back to the table, where Alius was already sitting before the two Books. The Silver book sat unopened in front of her, the other in front of Simian, who looked anxious. Adrian read his expression as the sense of being unprepared that he felt when he had taken exams in school.

"Good morning, Simian," said Adrian.

"Good morning to you," smiled the Jamaican. Sammy stood directly behind his chair, staring reverently over his uncle's shoulder at the Golden Book.

Adrian sat down next to Alius and touched the cover of the Book of Wisdoms. It seemed a long time since he last read from these Books.

Ester provided black diamond pendants on golden chains to absorb the dark energies from the silver Book of Knowledge.

Ponte, stepped forward and said, "Simian, please open your book."

Simian reached out and bent a finger under the heavy cover. He turned it over and stared at the figures wandering around the glassy pages, then looked up at Adrian and Alius with a quizzical look.

"You must ask a question," said Adrian. "Ask whether there is a Green Crystal on the Island of Jamaica."

"Is there a mighty Green Crystal in Jamaica?"

The figures marched around the pages and bounced off the edges, before they finally formed the word 'Yes'.

Simian looked up in amazement, "It says 'Yes'!"

Adrian winked at the Professor. "I think that we've found another one!"

Ponte smiled and turned his gaze to Sammy, who was still staring at the pages. "I don't see anything. The figures just seem to move around and around."

Ponte sighed, "Only a true *seer* can see the messages that appear in this book. I've plied these texts for years and I can't see anything either."

"Does this mean that I am not a *seer*?" asked Sammy.

"I'm afraid so. Simian, on the other hand, seems to have the talent. We will begin training you as soon as possible." He placed a pudgy hand on Sammy's shoulder, "Don't be disappointed. The *seers* interpret the Books but the rest of us work with that information to create and control the magic of this island. We will train you as a Keeper of the Powers."

Sammy smiled reluctantly.

Simian again stared at the book and asked, "Am I descended from Protus?"

"Yes."

"Is there a Black Crystal in Jamaica?"

"Yes"

"Where?"

A map appeared with a black diamond off the northeast coast. The tome pulsed, "Its power is increasing."

Simian glanced at Adrian and Alius, then turned to the Professor. "What does it mean?"

"We're not sure, yet, and that's why I've asked Adrian and Alius to work with us today. We have many questions," said Ponte, without his usual smile.

Simian rose from the table and Adrian sat down in his place. There was a pounding at the door and Nanchez strode through the parlor, "Good morning to ya'!"

It was late in the afternoon when Ester made that sound in her throat and demanded that Nanchez and Ponte stop peppering the *seers* with questions. Sammy and Simian had been silent throughout the process. Sitting in chairs at either end of the table, they watched the two men wander about the room as Alius and Adrian probed the Texts for information about the differences between the vectors that connected the positive and negative Crystals.

"Right you are," said Ponte, impatiently. "We'll continue tomorrow."

"I'm so tired," moaned Alius, as she closed the cover to the Book of Knowledge. "I need to go outside before the sun disappears!"

Sammy joined the two *seers*, as they walked out through the front door into long shadows cast by the sun setting behind the ridge. "I'm not sure I understand what was happening in there. It seems that the work you're doing is very hard."

"It's tedious and exhausting," replied Adrian with a yawn. "Especially, when we don't know what we're looking for or why they're stepping through this process." He turned to face the sun and stretched.

"I get the feeling that there's something unusual about the vectors from the Black Crystal," said Alius. "The one thing I did learn was that the vectors from the two Crystals are different. It seems they're separate and distinct, yet they overlap. The other thing I realized is that there has been a change in the power that's being generated by the Black Crystal. It's increasing and Nanchez and the Professor don't know why."

Adrian sighed, "Maybe we'll learn more tomorrow. At some point, they're going to have to share their thoughts, if we're ever going to find the answers they're seeking. This process will only give us half the answers. They have to trust us enough to allow us to explore the Texts on a deeper level."

Sammy smiled, "Perhaps I do not wish to be a *seer?*"

"It's a special gift but, when I learned I was a *seer*, Tic told me that 'understanding is demanding,' that this ability involves a huge responsibility and you're seeing part of that burden. There's nothing exciting about what we're doing but there's no giving up until we find the morsel the Keepers are looking for. Don't be disappointed that you didn't inherit the talent. Professor Ponte knows more than we might ever learn and the things that you'll discover through him are of more practical value than what we know. He can transform the information we find into real uses and see how different pieces fit together," said Adrian.

"It's almost as if we're conduits gushing information and he's the interpreter," smiled Alius. "If you're willing to work hard, your part will be of great value to your people. Be patient with him and with yourself. Oh, and you might have noticed that he's a weird combination of mad scientist and mischievous little kid in that chubby body but he's got a huge heart."

Sammy smiled, "I'm ready to learn."

After dinner, Adrian wandered into the girls' room to find them lying on their beds watching cartoons. He sat down on the floor and stared at the animation floating in front of the *messenger*.

He was tired and his mind kept going back to the questions that the Professor and Nanchez had been asking throughout most of the day. Neither of the Keepers offered an explanation for their inquiries but they kept going back to the unique qualities of the vectors that connected the Black Crystals.

He tried to focus on the *messenger* but really had no idea of what was happening. Finally, he turned to Molly and asked, "Do you get news?"

"Sure," she replied.

"Could we watch the headlines? I feel like we've been on another planet."

"Yeah, this is boring," she said. "NEWS!"

The cartoon on the *messenger* blurred out and was replaced by a beautiful blond woman, with huge blue eyes and too much makeup, reading the news headlines in front of a map of the world. Adrian was so tired that he only picked up bits of phrases the announcer was saying. "Bombings in Paris... Another massacre in central Africa...U.S. troops...a coup in Argentina...Israel and Palestine again failed to reach agreement...suicide bombing in Bali...protests in Saudi Arabia...another blow to the U.S. economy...European and Japanese markets were down for the week...the Pope fell ill today..."

Megan moaned, "This is depressing. Let's watch something else."

Adrian said, "Fine, I can't keep track of what she's saying anyway." He wandered out through the hallway, into his own room, and flopped on the bed. As he dozed off, his mind kept moving from one fragment of thought to another...*seers working with Black Crystals, tragedies and conflicts across the globe, Black vectors...The Books...*

He was roused as his Father sat gently on the edge of the bed, balancing an *orb* in his hand, "You're not tired are you?"

"I'm exhausted. The Professor and Nanchez hammered us with questions all day and the process is draining. I hope they give us a break tomorrow."

"Well, we're supposed to have a meeting with the elders about the things we learned on the Island of the Children and talk about how we could incorporate their technologies here. It should last until after lunch, so you're probably off the hook for at least part of the day."

"Good."

"Aunt Elsie is serving up some warm cherry pie and ice cream in the kitchen. Would you like some?"

"Sure," replied Adrian in a whisper. He rolled out of bed and shuffled after his father down the stairs to the kitchen. The family was gathered around the oval table and Brandy's muzzle was covered with ice cream from a bowl on the floor.

"Hi Brandy!" exclaimed Adrian, as he knelt to pet the Irish setter. "It's nice to be home."

"It sure is. I didn't mind the boat trip, and I actually got used to the sway of the boat, but it's nice to sleep on my own little pallet and sneak some ice cream from my favorite neighbors!"

"Without you and Tic, we might never have found my parents or chased the pirates away. I want to thank you once more, just so you know how grateful I am."

Brandy licked the cream from his muzzle and looked directly into Adrian's eyes, "You've done so much to preserve our way of life and to overcome evil in such a short time. It's been our honor to help and we're ready to go again, if you need us."

Adrian wrapped his arms around the red dog and nestled against his soft fur, then walked over to the table and sat down between the girls, who were giggling about some inside joke that he missed. The cherry pie was delicious, even better with freshly made ice cream. He looked around the table and realized that these were the most important people in the world to him and he felt safe and warm in their company. Home was Morgan's Knot and The House of the Four Seasons.

Chapter 5

Sara and Elsie were busy serving eggs, fish, toast, fried potatoes, muffins, and fresh fruit, when Adrian wandered into the kitchen the next morning. His body felt better but his mind was still tired. Molly and Megan sat down just as his mother placed a plate in front of him.

"Let's go to the forest today!" said Megan.

"That would be lovely," replied Adrian. "We should take Sammy and Alius."

"I'll call them and the rest of the kids after breakfast," said Molly.

Elsie brought two more plates to the table, "I'll make a basket to take with you. We're all going to the meeting this morning, so you could take the wagon, if you like."

"That would be great!"

John and George came in from the barn just as the children were leaving the table, lingering long enough to hug their fathers, before scampering off to George's study to call their friends.

An hour later, Ponte pulled up in the yard in his crazy red wagon with the yellow fringe around the top. This time Sammy was gleefully honking the horn with Alius and Ponte holding their hands over their ears and egging him on.

"Enough already!" cried Alius.

With one final toot, Sammy giggled and climbed out of the strange contraption, as Adrian and the girls ran down the steps. "Good morning!"

"It is a lovely morning. You'll like the forest, it's the best place to understand The Balance," replied Adrian.

Alius jumped out of the back of the wagon and walked around to greet her friends. She looked as tired as Adrian felt.

The Professor greeted Molly and Megan, then turned to the two *seers*. "I know we pushed you two pretty hard yesterday and I just want you to know how much I appreciate your effort."

"We both want to help in any way we can but it might be easier if we knew what we were looking for…and why," said Adrian.

"You're right and I apologize for not being more forthcoming. When we have some time, I'll explain what we've learned and what we don't know. In the meantime, enjoy your day in the forest, you deserve the respite!"

"Have you had a chance to talk with Simian about how he transports himself across the vectors?"

"Yes, we've touched on it and I'm hoping that we'll have more time this evening. I've a feeling this meeting is going to take all day and we're taking him along to introduce him to our friends and our magic. We're hoping that he'll have a slightly different perspective into the powers that he's discovered and how they might be applied here."

"Are you going to discuss the underworld and the diving suits?"

"Yes, we'll certainly talk about all of that and I'm hoping we can start incorporating some of what we learned to expand our use of the powers on the island. Who knows, maybe an undersea city would be beneficial here. We'll see what everyone thinks," smiled Ponte. "I'm off. I have to pick up Ester and Simian and I want to meet with Jofre, Mandor, and Nanchez before we begin. Would you two be willing to read from the Books again tomorrow?"

Adrian and Alius glanced at each other and sighed, "Sure."

"Right then, have fun in the forest!" said Ponte, as he climbed into the wagon, honked the horn several times, and roared off through the gate in a plume of dust.

The children ran into the house, kissed their parents, grabbed the basket that Elsie and Sara had prepared, and moved like a small herd to the barn. Molly and Megan were arguing about who was going to drive.

"How about if I drive us down there and you two can figure out who's driving back?" asked Adrian.

"Okay," replied the girls. Adrian got the feeling that the argument was half the fun.

"The rest of the kids will meet us there," said Molly, as she climbed into the back of the wagon with Megan and Sammy.

Alius settled into the bench seat in the front with Adrian and said, "I have a surprise for you but I won't tell you what it is until we get there!"

"A surprise?"

Alius smiled, "Yeah, you'll like this one!"

Adrian pulled the wagon out of the barn and headed south on the path. They passed the bluff above their favorite beach, through fields lush with growth, stopping to sample luscious peaches along the way, and, finally, parked near the path into the forest.

Flocks of birds appeared out of the foliage and swarmed around the children as they trotted into the woods. Sammy looked up into the tall trees and the birds flying around above his head, "This is fairly magical. Jamaica is beautiful but we have nothing like this!"

Molly took his hand and led him along the path. "Oh, this is just the beginning. Just wait, the brook is just ahead!"

Presently, they came to the stream and found the other children sitting with Beggar the Bear, Daphne, the beautiful deer, her foal and her mate, Dante, raccoons, squirrels, chipmunks, two fox, a mountain lion, and Brandy, who was submerged in the cool water, save his eyes and nose.

Morgan and Kelly ran up the path to greet the new arrivals. Josh and Ian were perched on a large rock, feeding dried corn to the smaller animals and offering the occasional cookie to Beggar.

The animals welcomed their friends and Daphne moved to nuzzle with Adrian. "We hear you saved another island!"

"Well, with a lot of help from my friends here and Tic and Brandy, of course. We worked with a boatload of circus animals and a troupe of children, so they did the hard parts."

"We're glad you're back!"

The children settled on the rocks on the banks of the little stream. Beggar wandered over and sat down next to Sammy. "You're new here and you look different than everyone else. What's your name?"

Sammy looked up at his new friends with an expression of pure wonder, "I'm Sammy, I'm from Jamaica, and I'm pleased to meet you."

Beggar sniffed his pockets and licked his cheek with woeful eyes, "They call me Beggar. You don't have anything for me to eat do you?"

Molly cried, "Beggar, leave him alone! All the food is in these baskets and I'm going to guard them, so you don't steal it all!"

"Ahhh," moaned Beggar. "It was worth a try."

Sammy hugged the little bear and shared a cookie. "This is magic!"

"Yes, it is…and this is the way it should be in the rest of the world," said Adrian.

Morgan waded through the stream to sit next to Adrian, "Are you feeling better?"

"Yes, thank you. I'm sorry that I was so depressed when we talked the other day. Just being here with all of you and the animals is enough to remind me of why I did the things that I had to do to save all of this. You're right, I can't go back to being the boy that I was when I arrived here but I have to admit that I miss the simplicity or, maybe, the innocence of life before Morgan's Knot."

"I know," smiled Morgan. "But I'm glad that you are the person you are."

Just then a deep whooshing followed a great shadow that soared above his head and Magnus settled down on the rock next to the young *seer*. Alius smiled, "I told you I had a surprise for you!"

"Magnus! It's so good to see you."

"It's nice to be home and, now, I don't have to worry about flying over the mountain. They don't shoot at me anymore!"

"That's as it should be!"

Adrian wrapped an arm around the big bird's wings and gave him a hug. "I sure appreciate your help on the Island of the Children."

The huge eagle fluffed his feathers and squawked, "I got to visit the Pacific and I didn't have to fly all the way there or back!" Everyone laughed together.

He pecked at the boy's ear, "I have a question."

Adrian turned to the giant bird, "Okay."

"You know that we, meaning the animals and the birds...the natural creatures, all know when a storm is coming by the change in the pressure. We know when there's going to be an earthquake because we can feel the vibrations long before humans or their sensors can pick it up. On the island, we are all keenly aware of the vectors. It's not that we can see them but rather that we feel the energy, when we pass through them or travel along their path. The waves from the mountain are cold and violent while those coming from beneath the observatory are warm and smooth."

"I think I understand," replied Adrian with a curious look.

"Well, since we got back, when I fly near the mountain, I am aware of a change in the energies being emitted by the Black Crystal. It is far more intense than it was before we left." The beautiful bird, looking down his beak, reminded Adrian of George gazing intently through his little glasses.

"That's interesting because the Professor and Nanchez have been asking a lot of questions about the vectors, through us, in the Book of Wisdoms. I honestly don't know what's going on but I'll find out tomorrow."

"I hope this information is helpful."

"Believe me, it is."

More animals joined the party and the children played through the morning into the early afternoon. Adrian sat down next to Sammy, while they ate the peanut butter and honey sandwiches that Elsie and Sara had placed in the baskets.

"I understand," said Sammy, as birds swarmed around his outstretched hand, picking up crumbs of bread from his sandwich. "This is beyond belief!"

"As I said, this is the way it should be all over the world. When you see what can be, then you understand why we have to dedicate our lives to preserving and expanding this way of life. The people of this island have worked for generations to make this possible. It is The Balance."

"I am almost embarrassed that I didn't understand this wonder before, in spite of all that my Uncle Simian tried to teach me and so many magical things happening all around, I was too blind or preoccupied to really take it all in."

"I know exactly how you feel, it was right in front of us and we didn't see it until we got a chance to experience the friendship," smiled Adrian. "This is why you must accept the Professor's offer to teach you to be a Keeper of the Powers. You might not be a *seer* but you can contribute a great deal to The Balance in Jamaica and throughout the world."

"I see what you mean," replied Sammy quietly. "I have to admit that I was disappointed that I could not read from your Golden Book but, after these few hours with these wonderful creatures, I want to learn everything I can. I will become a Keeper!"

Chapter 6

George, Ponte, Ester, Sara, Dr. Stevens, Jofre, Mandor, and Nanchez sat in chairs on a small stage before the crowd of almost a thousand residents of the island.

George called the meeting to order and introduced Sara.

Adrian's Mother stood before her neighbors, "We're just back from being stranded and then rescued by Adrian and his friends from an island in the Pacific called La Isle de los Ninas, the Island of the Children. Its name is a long and complicated story. What we would like to explain is that the people of the island have harnessed the powers of a Ruby Crystal, much like ours, but their technology far surpasses anything that we've developed."

"They've built a city under the ocean. It's comprised of a series of glass domes connected by tunnels. They move about in the ocean, the way we move on land. Several of us and the seven children who made the trip have been trained to use sophisticated diving suits that allow divers to slip through the water at high speeds, remain at depth almost indefinitely, and work at everything from planting and harvesting underwater crops to constructing new domes."

There were murmurs in the crowd.

"My husband, John, George, Ponte, Travis, and I have received basic training in diving and the production of the diving suits, their construction techniques, and underwater farming. Ponte spent weeks with their Keeper, Dadeus, learning about their uses of the powers."

"We would like to propose that a committee be formed to explore how these technologies could benefit the residents of Morgan's Knot. Are there any questions?"

Hands shot into the air, "What use would we have for underwater farming? We grow everything that we need on the island."

"That's something that needs to be explored. In spite of the fact that the power of the vectors allows almost continuous production in our fields, what would happen if the population suddenly grew or a drought or some disease destroyed our crops? We see this as an extension of what we've been doing on the surface not a replacement. The undersea world is a wonderland and something that I hope each of you will get to experience."

"Tell us more about the domes!"

John stood to answer the question, "Their domes probably range from one hundred to three hundred meters in diameter and half that in height. They're made of pre-constructed beams that are connected together. The spaces between the supports are sealed with a thick glass membrane, so everyone inside can see the world around them. It's beautiful."

"What about oxygen, how do they ventilate the place?"

"They have a rather sophisticated system that separates water into oxygen and hydrogen and then mixes the oxygen with nitrogen and other gases to produce pure clean air. Since the pirates were driven away, they've started building a ventilation system to the surface of the island to supplement their air supply."

"Did you bring the diving suits back with you."

"Yes, we'll ask the children to demonstrate them for you, so you can see how they work," replied John.

Ponte rose from his chair, "Perhaps a picture is worth several thousand words! It is very hard to describe the place that we've been because there is nothing else like it anyplace in the world. We've developed the magic of the Crystals to provide for almost everything we need on this island. Once a month, our trawlers go out to fish but, beyond that, we are surrounded by an ocean that we know nothing about. It is a storehouse of potential and we would be foolish to continue to ignore it."

With that, he turned to a large *messenger* that projected a giant image on the wall of the meeting room. The Professor mashed a button and an image of Gabrielle appeared. "May I introduce our host on the Island of the Children, Gabrielle."

The crowd applauded.

Dressed in his blue robes, he looked into the camera with kind smiling eyes, "It's nice to see so much interest in the crowd that you've gathered. We've arranged a little video tour of our facilities. In spite of our lack of professional production, we hope it will introduce you to our world."

His image faded into a tight frame of schools of silver fish flashing through the glow of the *orbs* on the outside of the residential dome. The camera pulled back to reveal a wide view of the open space and the glass panels opening to the undersea world. It panned to show terraced entrances to the apartments that wrapped around the back of the dome. "These are our residential apartments. Each has full accommodations for a small family, although we share our meals in the dining dome not far from here, and the walls and ceilings are made of this same glass forms, so the life of the ocean is always just outside."

The camera zoomed out through one of the windows. The audience could see the construction crews working on the next dome, the air bubbles around their suits shimmering in the light of powerful *orbs* bathing the site. The new sphere was nearing completion, save the last three panels. "As you can see, our construction team is almost finished with the structure for the next dome. We should have it sealed in the next few weeks. Also, notice that our building technique is fairly simple, we don't want to endanger the crew!"

The camera swept down to a reef meandering along just outside the windows. Several sharks cruised through the frame, as schools of brilliant blue and yellow angle fish scattered in search of shelter. Sea fans swayed in the currents and a stingray sprang out of the sand and rolled over backwards to 'oooohhs'…and 'aaahhhhs' from the crowd.

Whoever was running the video pulled back and moved through a glass tunnel to the access dome, where several divers were just entering the water. Soule turned and walked up to the camera. "Hi, my name is

Soule and I teach our residents to dive. These special suits allow us to move through the water at high speeds and, at the same time, allow maximum dexterity. We can work at depth for hours on end. We'd love to teach all of you!"

Soule pulled the headpiece over his face and turned to rejoin the group of divers. The gray aliens waved to the camera, slowly descended down the ramp into the water, and cruised out through the interface.

Gabrielle appeared before the lens again, "In just a moment, we'll show you a view of our underwater farm. We've harvested everything that we could possibly need from the ocean for years without killing a single fish. As our friends can attest, our menu is delicious!"

The camera moved to the window where fields of greens swayed slowly back and forth with the ebb and flow of the currents. Lobsters and crabs roamed through the produce and small fish pecked away tiny creatures that might injure the plants.

Gabrielle stepped into the foreground, "There is a Balance beneath the surface of the sea, just as there is a Balance on Morgan's Knot. We invite you to consider the possibilities of expanding your world to include life under the ocean. If any of you would like to come for a visit, we would welcome you as our guests. If you decide to move forward with developing structures in the sea, we will be happy to come and guide you through the process."

"I thank you for your time and blessings to Ponte, George, John, Sara, Travis, and the children. We miss you!"

The picture faded and the audience applauded.

Ponte waited for the crowd to quiet, "As you can see, there is a world that we've never considered before. There are technologies that could benefit our community and our way of life. Now that the North and the South have joined together, we have more than enough manpower, if you'll excuse that expression ladies, to do much more to extend the magic of this island."

The meeting continued for hours, as the residents asked enthusiastic questions and made positive proposals.

Chapter 7

Zepallo stood before a raised console at the center of a huge cavern that had been carved into the bowels of a mountain on a volcanic island in the middle of nowhere in the South Atlantic. Giant screens encircled rows of technicians working at computers unlike any in the world. Motorized chairs pivoted to allow a complete view of three-dimensional holograms surrounding the workers. Gloves, with sensors in the fingertips, and monocles, that tracked their eye movements, allowed multi-tasking on a grand scale.

Their individual assignments were projected onto the screens around the room, yet Zepallo was focused on a panel that displayed the news headlines. *"Bombings in Paris ...Another massacre in central Africa...U.S. troops...a coup in Argentina...Israel and Palestine again failed to reach agreement...a suicide bombing in Bali...protests in Saudi Arabia...another blow to the U.S. economy...European and Japanese markets are down...the Pope fell ill today..."*

Zepallo's slender lips curled into an evil scowl, as he turned to his second-in-command, "Step by step, they do our bidding for us!"

Sir Winston, as Zepallo referred to his associate, was tall, lean, and weathered. His perfectly quaffed silver hair and goatee framed dark beady eyes that tended to glare down a long, slender nose at those beneath him with impatience and distain. His manner made no attempt to conceal unabashed arrogance born of an aristocratic station and he was known to have great influence, behind the scenes, in the British financial world. He spoke with slow deliberation, each word considered before it passed his pursed lips.

"It is as you predicted, Sire, and we have only initiated the primary phase of your plan. As these technicians make the necessary connections and our emissaries fulfill their directives, our strategy will unfold throughout the world."

They turned to a map of the globe covered with glowing dots, half black, half red. As each connection was completed, bridges between the black dots were added to the display. Because the Black Crystals were spread across the planet, each had to be fixed to those around it, forming a web of links. Those surrounding the Atlantic were first and the web extended from this secret command center to the North Pole. As each Crystal was added, the energy it created could be directed from this room. Gradually, the network would extend east and west until a net covered the Earth and the Powers, the Black Powers, could be merged.

Once the operation was concluded, every electronic transmission and every electrical system could be monitored and controlled. Messages sent through telephones, cell phones, computers, the Internet, and satellite transmissions would pass through this command center, where they could be recorded and analyzed or scrambled and replaced. The power grid in every country in the world could be turned on or off at the will of the Dark Lord, at the behest of the Council of Ollapez, and that was only the beginning.

The net of connections between the Black Crystals used a frequency that was unknown to the world's scientists and, because the web of links would span the entire globe, there would be no way to trace the interference to this facility beneath an ice-covered lump of rock.

Chapter 8

Adrian sat on the kitchen steps with his mother, sipping a cup of warm tea. "How did your meeting go?"

"It was interesting to see the reaction to what we'd learned and the benefits of adding some of their technology into our systems here. Even though most of us grew up understanding the benefits of the powers of the Crystals, there was a little bit of disbelief from some people at first. Somehow, Ponte managed to provide a connection to Gabrielle and a video tour of the domes. It was quite remarkable. In the end, everyone agreed to explore the possibility of adding an undersea compound. Everyone wants to see how the diving suits work and I think that we'll begin producing our own suits very soon. We're ordering the materials that we don't have from the mainland and the special features will come from the Island of the Children."

"If I didn't know better, I'd probably doubt our stories too, so, I can understand how some people might not believe the things we encountered."

"Well, we hope that all of you can demonstrate the suits in the next few days."

"Oh, I'd love to. I've missed the ocean, well at least the part that we can't see from the surface!" giggled Adrian. "I think I've had enough yachting for a while!"

"The other thing that was decided was that we should have a harvest festival. Everyone on the island has a lot to be thankful for."

"That's a wonderful idea. When will it be?"

"Next weekend. Elsie's already started planning the menu!"

Adrian hugged his Mother and leaned back against the step. It was good to be home.

Adrian, Alius, Sammy, Ponte, Ester, and Simian sat at the table in the Professor's dining room. Alius had started working with Simian and the Golden Book and he was beginning to understand the depth of information that could be gleaned from the Texts.

"Moving along the vectors isn't hard," said Simian. "It's a matter of concentrating on the vibrations that are being sent out by the Crystals. They follow very distinct paths, skipping from one point to another. We know that the House of the Four Seasons sits on a power point, as does Dr. Stevens' and other places on the island. The first thing that you have to do is to allow your mind to hear the vibrations. It is almost like a sound that you hear in your very core without using your ears."

"I know that sound. I heard it while I was inside the Crystal," commented Adrian. "It's like a low rumbling hum."

"That's it!" replied Simian. "Can you hear it now?"

Adrian closed his eyes and concentrated. In the depths of his being, he could feel a deep tremor. It grew louder as he focused his mind, "I hear it."

"Have faith in the power of the Crystals and your belief in The Balance. From what I am learning, we're riding the vibrations of the positive Crystals. I'm not sure what would happen if we were to try to follow the energy of the Black Crystal. I can see the avenues of the dark vectors but I'm not sure that any of us are ready to try that." His eyes glistened like the moon over the ocean when he laughed.

"Now, let's concentrate on your destination. We'll start with something simple. The path of the vector to the House of the Four Seasons also passes through the Professor's parlor. See the room in your mind. See it with absolute clarity because you have to know where you are going to land before you begin this process. Otherwise, you might end up in a wall or beneath a stone."

Adrian closed his eyes and concentrated on the parlor. He could see the furniture, the struggling embers in the fireplace, and the front door. He focused on the couch next to the fireplace. The vibration grew louder, until it was almost deafening. He heard a loud whoosh and a rush of colored lights flowing past in a blaze of electric streamers. Suddenly, he felt something soft under his bottom, instead of the stiff wooden chair at the table in the dining room, and he heard a loud shriek.

Adrian opened his eyes and found himself sitting on the couch in the parlor, face to face with Tic, who was straddling the back of the sofa with every hair on his body standing on end, his claws fully extended, and his dark eyes wide with panic.

"Don't do that!" screeched Tic.

Adrian reached up and took the cat in his arms, "I'm sorry I startled you but that was incredible!"

"That's all well and good, but give a cat some warning!"

Adrian stood up and put Tic back on the couch with a gentle pet. He felt mildly dizzy and slowly shuffled back to the table and sat down.

Simian smiled, "Well done!"

Adrian looked at Sammy, "Can you do this?"

"No. I can travel on the paths if Simian is touching me but I'm afraid that I can't hear the vibrations."

"I wonder whether this is another of those things that only a *seer* can do?"

Simian turned to Ponte, "Can you hear the tone?"

"I don't think so. I couldn't even hear the voice that Adrian talked about hearing as he entered the Crystal," replied Ponte.

"Perhaps I will have to take you along the vector to see if you can hear it?"

"I'd love to try it out!"

"Well, first, let us give Miss Alius a go. Would you like to try?"

Alius grinned, "Sure!"

"Alright, clear your mind of all thoughts and emotions and listen to the tone that is being produced by the energy of the Crystal."

Everyone was silent for a few moments before Simian said softly, "Do you hear a low rumble?"

"Yes," replied Alius with a little smirk.

"Now concentrate on the parlor but let's pick the burgundy chair in front of the fireplace, so we don't scare the cat," said Simian very quietly. "See the room, see the chair, see yourself sitting in the chair."

Suddenly, there was a whoosh and Alius was sitting in the chair before the hearth. She opened her eyes and turned to the group in the dining room with a broad smile. "I did it!"

She stood up and reached for the back of the chair, "You didn't tell me that it would make me dizzy!"

"Just hold on for a moment, your mind will clear," said Simian.

Alius walked slowly back to sit down at the table. "That's amazing. I want to go farther!"

"All in good time. Let me take the Professor for a little ride. You children go outside and we'll meet you on the path."

Adrian, Alius, Ester, and Sammy walked out the front door and waited. Presently, they heard the rush and Simian and the Professor were standing at the gate in the path leading up to the observatory. Ponte giggled like a schoolboy who had just pulled off a prank under the nose of his least favorite teacher. "Oh, that was wonderful. I understand what Alius meant, I want to go farther!"

"Did you hear the sound?"

"No, I saw lights flashing past and I heard the whoosh but I didn't hear a tone," replied the Professor.

"Well, that establishes the premise that only a *seer* can travel along the paths. Let us return to the dining room." He reached up and touched Ester on the shoulder and, before she could react, they disappeared.

Ponte snickered as they skipped up the steps and through the front door to find the two of them sitting at the table, Ester smiling and Simian cackling, "I'm sorry, I should have asked your permission but I couldn't resist!"

"That's quite alright, what a wonderful sensation!"

Everyone sat down and Simian said, "Alius, I'm afraid that I am not quite sure about using the vector that has been set up between the Golden Crystal and the Black Crystal in the mountain. I need to test it for safety, so I'm afraid that you'll have to return home in the Professor's trolley but I would like to see if Adrian can move himself back to the House of the Four Seasons. Would you like to try?"

"Sure!"

The Professor interrupted, "If you're leaving us, would you be kind enough to come back tomorrow morning? We have some questions for the Books."

"I'll be here after breakfast."

"Okay, concentrate and listen. Have faith in the powers and The Balance…and yourself. See where you want to land and listen for the tone…" whispered Simian.

A few moments later, Adrian vanished. Simian closed his eyes and concentrated. "He's in the kitchen. I think his aunt's reaction was worse than Tic's!"

Adrian felt himself moving through space and saw the flowing colors streaming past like shards of a shattered rainbow. He heard the hum of the vibrations and kept focusing on the middle of the kitchen. He heard a clatter and a loud scream as he landed. Elsie, standing at the sink washing dishes, dropped a platter on the floor as Adrian materialized behind her.

"Where did you come from?"

"The Professor's. Simian is teaching us how to travel along the vectors!"

"Well, give your poor aunt some warning before you do that. You scared the life out of me!"

Adrian blushed and hugged his aunt, "I'm sorry!"

Sara, John, George, and the girls rushed into the kitchen. "What happened?" asked Sara.

"Your son just materialized out of thin air and scared me to death. It's not everyday that someone drops out of nowhere!"

Everyone looked at Adrian. "I'm sorry. I really didn't mean to scare you. We were practicing moving along the vectors and Simian decided that I was ready to try a longer distance, so here I am!"

Molly and Megan squinted their eyes in disbelief. "Are you joking?"

"No, I'm serious. Remember when Simian took me to the Crystal in Jamaica? Well, he's teaching us the technique. Unfortunately, it seems that only *seers* can do it. He took the Professor, from the dining room to the path outside the observatory, and he loved it."

Everyone was quiet for a moment, staring at Adrian with bewildered expressions. The young *seer* picked up the platter from the floor and gave his aunt another hug, "I'm sorry I scared you."

"Oh, that's alright. Just when I think I understand about the powers of *seers*, you come up with something new!"

Megan asked, "Can you take us with you?"

"I'm not sure that I'm ready for that yet but when I learn the a bit more, I'll be happy to take you."

"Promise?" asked Megan.

"Promise!"

Molly smiled, "Okay, now, I'm hungry. Do we have any of that peach ice cream left?"

"You're always hungry!" cried her sister.

The girls pulled the ice cream from the freezer and served bowls for everyone.

John stared at his son and finally said, "I get the feeling that the powers of the *seer* are not limited to reading from the Texts or organizing the animals. I'm proud of what you're learning and what you're doing but I have to admit that I worry about your safety."

"The one thing I've learned, since I found out I was a *seer*, is that there seem to be no limits to the powers of the Crystals. The people of the underworld on the Island of the Children use them in ways that no one ever considered here on Morgan's Knot. I wouldn't be surprised to find other places where people are using them in ways that we have yet to discover. I've no choice but to follow my path and learn everything I can. I know that someday, it will prove useful."

"I know, but every parent has the right to worry about their children. We are no different," smiled John, hugging his son.

Chapter 9

Adrian finished his breakfast, kissed his mother and Aunt Elsie, and walked out into the sunshine. The dew on the grasses shimmered in a gentle breeze that rustled fading leaves in the old oak and he turned to face the warmth of the sun in front of the garden. The vegetable patch was overflowing with produce and flowers. Bees buzzed from one bloom to the next and then back to the hives at the corners. Birds flew overhead and swooped down to collect bugs among the plantings and two tiny ruby-throated hummingbirds flitted about, chasing after each other in a high-speed game of tag.

Several cows, a few sheep and goats were wandering around the yard in front of the old barn. He gazed at the stone farmhouse and noticed that the roses beneath the windows were blooming bright orange and yellow. The trees to the west were just beginning to show hints of autumn color and the fields were a patchwork of mature crops.

He knew that it would be hours before he would see the sun again and he hesitated for a moment to savor the sensation. Finally, he closed his eyes and concentrated on the parlor in the Professor's house. He listened intently until he heard the low rumble of the vibrations of the vectors and willed himself along the path.

Moments later, he was standing in the living room at the observatory. Simian looked up with a smile from the dining room table and said, "You seem to have mastered the art of moving along the vectors!"

"My cousin wanted me to take her last night but I wasn't sure about my own technique. Can you teach me how to transport other people?"

"Sure, it's not hard. It just takes more energy and control," laughed Simian.

"Ahoy!" cried Alius marching through the front door in Nanchez' wake.

The group settled down around the table and Adrian placed his hands on the closed book in front of him, staring intently at Ponte. "Professor, I think we could be more direct in finding answers to your questions, if you'd let us in on what's going on. We're trying to interpret without knowing what we're looking for."

"I agree and I should apologize for not being more forthcoming," smiled Ponte. "It's just…complicated."

Nanchez nodded in agreement, "While you were away, I installed a vector between the Golden Crystal and the Black Crystal to balance the energy that we're drawing for all the systems we use on the island. Shortly before you got back from your tropical excursion, I noticed that the power being produced by the Black Crystal had increased substantially, although our consumption had not changed. For some reason, it's being drawn away from the island on a phantom vector and we have no idea where it's going or who is controlling this change."

Everyone was quiet for a few moments, as each pondered the challenge and the possible consequences of any action they might take.

Finally, Adrian looked up and said, "I spent a lot of time thinking about the Books and the powers, on our way back from Jamaica. After learning about the systems they've developed on the Island of the Children and seeing the Green Crystal on Jamaica, I wondered about whether there are other people around the world who are using the Crystals in ways that we've never considered. I also wondered about people who might be using the Black Crystals, just as you did before the…reunion, only on a bigger scale."

Everyone was gaping, so he continued, "We've learned that all of the Positive Crystals are loosely connected by vectors that cover the globe but we have no idea whether the Black Crystals are connected in a similar way. What if someone was linking those vectors to all the Black Crystals?"

Nanchez' mouth dropped open, grasping the obvious, "As horrific as the thought might be, you might be on to something there. We could run a test through the Black Crystal to see where the dark vectors intersect and, perhaps, find a clue to where the power's going!"

Ponte interjected, "We should get in touch with Dadeus and have him run a similar investigation from his end to see whether power is fluctuating in their Black Crystal!"

Alius said quietly, "The first question for the Books is whether all of the Crystals are connected or whether there are two independent systems...one positive and the other negative."

The young *seers* opened the Books simultaneously. Alius fingered the black diamond pendant and asked, "Are all the Black Crystals connected together?"

The figures rushed around the pages before replying, "Not yet."

Simian leaned over Alius' shoulder and stared at the response, "That does not answer our question. Ask it whether all of the Positive Crystals are connected."

Adrian posed the question.

"No."

"Are all of the Black Crystals connected together?

"Not yet."

"Are some of the Black Crystals connected together?"

"Yes."

"Are the vectors for the Black Crystals and the vectors for the Positive Crystals connected together?"

"A few."

"Are there two structures?"

"Yes."

"Are the two systems independent of each other?"

"Yes, one balances the other."

"Is there a point where the connections for the Black Crystals come together?"

"Yes."

"Where?"

"Ice Island."

"Who is controlling that system?"

The screen in the Silver Book turned black, then, 'The Dark Lord of Ollapez, Legio Obscurum.' Alius sat back in her chair and stared at the message, before reading it for the Keepers.

Everyone was silent until Ester said, "Legio Obscurum? That's Latin for 'Legion of Darkness'."

Finally, Adrian leaned forward and asked, "Who is the Dark Lord?"

"Zepallo."

"Who is Zepallo?"

There was no response. Ponte pondered, mumbling under his breath, "We know that, throughout history, those who tapped into the powers of the Black Crystals used those energies to grab power to promote their own individual brand of evil. Germany during World War II, Cambodia during and after the Vietnam War, Iraq, Central Africa…the examples go on and on. My interpretation of what we have just learned is that someone named Zepallo is trying to do it again and, perhaps, on a larger and far more perilous scale."

Alius leaned forward and asked, "Where is Zepallo?"

"Ice Island."

"Is Zepallo a *seer*?"

"Yes."

"Does he have a Book of Wisdoms?"

A black box appeared. The little blond *seer* whispered, "A Black Book."

Alius and Adrian glanced around the table at each of their elders for some explanation.

Simian spoke first, "This is a dangerous and powerful man. We have much to learn."

"And we'd best find out what's going on in a hurry," said Nanchez. "Ponte, you get in touch with Dadeus and tell him what we've learned. See whether they've seen any disruption of their systems and whether they can run a test on the vectors from their end. I'll go back to the mountain and run a trace on the Black vectors to see if we can understand where the power is going. I'll take Sammy with me. It'll be a good opportunity for you to learn about our methods."

The little Jamaican straightened up but Ester added, "We need to find out who this Zepallo person is, he's the key to the mystery."

Ponte turned to the children, "I agree. We'll find out what we can and get back to you in a few hours. I'll take Simian with me to call Dadeus."

Adrian stood, "We'll be at the House of the Four Seasons. Call us when you're ready and we'll come back."

The group dispersed and Adrian and Alius walked outside into the sunshine and sat down on the grass. Alius took his hand and they stared silently out over the fields, lost in the realization that sinister enemies, employing the Dark Energies on a magnitude beyond comprehension, could be concealed on some remote ice-covered island not far beyond the horizon.

"You faced a lot of challenges in your quest for this island and chasing the pirates away from the Island of the Children," said Alius quietly. "This is on a different scale. This is about someone who wants to rule the world and has the means to make it happen!"

"I know…but I don't know what to do about it. The one thing I have to believe is that the powers of the Positive Crystals and The Balance are far more powerful than any other energy on the planet. There is an answer. We just have to find it."

"We will."

"Let's go to the House of the Four Seasons. I want to talk with George and my father about all of this."

"Okay."

The two *seers* grasped hands, closed their eyes, and concentrated on the yard in front of the garden. With a whoosh, they were gone.

Chapter 10

Adrian and Alius materialized in the yard near the garden. Elsie and the girls were busy harvesting vegetables and turned just in time to see the two *seers* appear.

Elsie smirked, "Will you stop doing that!"

The twins chimed in, "That looks like so much fun, we want to go!"

"We didn't mean to startle you. Are my Dad and George around?" asked Adrian.

"They're in the barn," said Elsie as she turned back to the garden, shaking her head.

Alius and Adrian walked up the path to find the two men's legs extended from beneath the wagon. Light, creeping through cracks between the wallboards, made dust in the air glisten like long luminous fingers igniting the darkness at the back of the barn.

"What are you doing?" asked Adrian, as his eyes traced along the wall, where George's tools were neatly hung above a long worn workbench.

"Just a little fine tuning. Your Aunt Elsie seems to think there's a vibration in the wagon," said John. "What are you doing here? I thought you were working with the Professor."

"We were but we've come across something disturbing and we wanted to talk with you about what we found."

"Okay."

The two men slid out from under the trolley, brushed dirt from their backsides and grease from their forearms, and stood to face the *seers*, "What do you want to talk about?"

Adrian explained the potential of what they found in the Books and the concerns of Ponte and Nanchez. He ended by saying, "We

found a person named Zepallo who is controlling this process and he
lives on an Ice Island."

"I was good in geography but that name doesn't ring any bells
for me. How about you?"

John thought for a moment and replied, "I've sailed all over the
planet and never heard that name before, either, but that doesn't mean
anything. Do you know where this Ice Island is located?"

"No."

George looked down at Adrian through his little glasses, "Ponte
is contacting Dadeus and Nanchez is checking the Black Vectors?"

"Yes, they said that they'll be in touch with us as soon as they
learn something new," replied Alius.

"I have to get in touch with Gabrielle this afternoon," said
George. "We'll see what he has to say."

Frustrated, the two *seers* sauntered into the sunshine and back to
the vegetable garden to help with the harvest.

After lunch, Adrian, Alius, Sara, John, and the twins crammed
into the small study as George dialed up the Island of the Children on
the *messenger*. The dimly lit room glowed in the radiance of a hologram of
Gabrielle's face surrounding the screen.

"George! How are you?"

"We're all fine. It's nice to be home. How are things
progressing?"

"The new fields are coming up nicely and we've just received our
first shipment of stone. We've cleaned up the plaza and the remains of
the buildings and now we're working on drawings of how each building
must have looked when they were first constructed. We'll attempt to
duplicate our forefathers' artistry and craftsmanship."

Adrian stepped in front of the screen and said, "How are all of
our friends? Raffe and Mary?"

"Raffe is advancing very quickly. He's learning to read from the Texts faster than from normal books. We've almost finished construction in the pyramid and should have it ready for students in the next few weeks."

George interrupted, "Gabrielle, I understand that Ponte spoke with Dadeus earlier in the day. It seems that we're having some interference in the power being produced by the Black Crystal. Have you had any similar fluctuations?"

"No. Dadeus was a bit miffed at the hour of the call but he's checked his instruments and doesn't see any changes on this end."

"Tell me, have you ever heard the name Zepallo?" asked George.

"Zepallo? No, I can't say that I have."

"Adrian and Alius have been reading from the Books and found a reference to that name and the problems with the Black Crystal. They say he's supposed to live on an Ice Island."

"Now that's interesting. Probably near one of the poles. Unfortunately, if a Crystal exists there, the island probably doesn't show up on any normal maps."

"I agree," replied George.

There was a commotion on the other end of the vector and Raffe and Mary appeared on either side of Gabrielle. "How are you?" asked Raffe.

"We're all fine," smiled Adrian. "We're trying to figure out why our Black Crystal is producing excess energy and where the power is going. We're studying the dark vectors and we've come across references to someone named Zepallo who lives on an Ice Island. We think they might be trying to connect the vectors all over the World."

"That's scary. Mary and I can check the Book of Natural Balance to see if we can find anything. Dadeus told us about talking with Ponte and he said that our systems seemed to be functioning normally."

"Let us know what you find."

"We'll get back to you," said Mary.

"It's good to know that all of you are well. Any sign of pirates?"

Gabrielle, Mary, and Raffe burst out laughing, "The latest word, from our suppliers on the mainland, is that the pirates believe the Island of the Children is haunted by aliens and ghosts. There've been no reports of piracy anywhere along the coast since our campaign."

"Good. Let's hope it stays that way!"

"We'll call you back later, after we check the Texts," said Mary.

"We'll talk with you then," said George as the hologram dissolved.

George turned to Adrian and Alius, "We could hope that the changes that we're seeing in the Black Crystal are unique to Morgan's Knot, but, from what you've told us, that might be wishful thinking. Keep us informed of what you learn. In the meantime, keep in mind that the power of the Positive Crystals and our faith in The Balance are far more robust than anything that can be produced through the Black Crystals."

Adrian and Alius nodded and turned to leave the room.

"One more thing," said George quietly. "We all have great faith in the two of you."

"Thank you," replied Alius.

Chapter 11

A dazzling orange sun was melting into the ridge to the west by the time the *seers* reconvened at the Professor's. Ester made a huge pot of soup, sandwiches, and a fruit salad and the group sat around the dining room table enjoying the meal and the latest scuttlebutt from around the island. A small reluctant fire crackled and spat in the fireplace in the parlor but the room was warm.

Ponte and Nanchez waited until everyone finished their supper before addressing the things they learned during the afternoon.

"We spoke with Dadeus and he's not seen any changes in the power being produced by their Black Crystal," said Ponte.

"We know," said Adrian. "We talked to Gabrielle, Mary, and Raffe earlier. Mary and Raffe are going to check in the Book of Natural Balance to see what they can find."

"Good, good," replied the Professor.

Nanchez rose from his chair and lumbered around the table, "Do you remember the bug I put on the Jasmine to track your movements?"

"Yes," replied Adrian.

"Well, I have a receiver in the workshop in the mountain and it appears that there are clusters of dark vectors that are connected together around the Atlantic. I can't tell where they all meet because they're chained together in clumps. I ran the same test on the Positive Crystals and found that they are loosely linked but there is no surge of power moving along their vectors. What I found most interesting is that the Positive vectors seem to be hooked together in clusters that overlap."

Adrian was quiet for a moment, "If someone is connecting the Black Crystals then perhaps the only power in the world that might be stronger would be connecting all of the Positive Crystals together. Is that possible?"

Ponte and Nanchez looked at each other. "I don't know the answer to your question," replied the Professor. "Perhaps we should consult the Texts."

Adrian and Alius brought the books to the table, donned black diamonds, and opened the glimmering covers. "Can all of the Positive Crystals be connected?"

"Yes."

"How can they be connected?"

"Through the nodes."

"What are nodes?"

"Points where the vectors from many Crystals overlap."

"How many are there?"

"Seven."

"Where are they?"

The figures roamed around the pages but did not form a response.

"Are the nodes connected to each other?"

"Not directly."

Alius asked, "Are there nodes that connect the Black Crystals?"

"No."

"Are they being connected individually?"

"Yes."

"Which Crystals are more powerful, the Positive or the Negative?"

The figures moved around the pages, bouncing off the edges and finally formed a golden diamond. Adrian and Alius glanced at each other and then to the rest of the group gathered around the table.

"There's an answer to this problem. We just need to ask the right questions," commented Nanchez.

Ponte and Nanchez peppered the *seers* with technical questions for several hours. Adrian and Alius probed the Books for deeper answers but they found no obvious solution to the puzzle.

Finally, Adrian looked up and said, "We know the Books hold the history of the Crystals and the people who worked with them through the centuries. I wonder whether they can tell us anything about the future?"

Alius pondered his thought for a moment, then asked the Book of Knowledge, "Is this the beginning of the end of times?"

The figures in the Books rushed around and around for several minutes before responding, "Conceivably."

"Can we stop it?"

"Yes."

"How?"

The figures moved about the pages in both books, "Break The Balance."

The *seers* stared at each other. "How?"

There was no response.

Adrian and Alius closed the Books and rose from the table, without comment. It was late and they were tired.

Ester broke the silence, "I think we all need to rest and think about what we've learned, which is considerable, mind you." She looked at Adrian, "The Books can only give us part of the answer to our questions."

Adrian stared at the floor for a long moment, "I think we need to find the right questions to ask The Books. I could enter the Golden Crystal but we don't yet know what to ask. That should be the last step."

Ponte patted the boy on the shoulder, "I've watched you enter the Crystals three times. Each time, I worried that you would not survive. I agree, that is our last choice, but it might be the only one that offers a solution to the problem. We're all tired and I agree with Ester, let's all get a good night's sleep. The festival is coming up this weekend and school starts next week. Perhaps you two should enjoy a few days off so that we can come together again with a fresh perspective."

"I agree. We're not at a crisis point yet and we know that the process of connecting the Black vectors will take some time," said Nanchez. "We've picked up some technical information that will take a few days to explore and analyze. Give us some time to work on this and we'll let you know what we find."

Everyone agreed and Alius left with Nanchez. Adrian concentrated on the vegetable garden at the House of the Four Seasons and, with a whoosh, disappeared.

———————

Endless chores, in preparation for the festival, filled the next few days. Elsie and Sara were firmly planted in the kitchen, sending the children to harvest vegetables from the garden and haul supplies from the cold cellar.

Adrian and Megan dragged a large basket of tomatoes up the kitchen steps and deposited them on the table. Sara turned to Adrian, "Thanks for bringing those in. I haven't been to a festival in years and this will be even more special because it will include everyone on the island. This should be fun!"

Adrian smiled. He enjoyed the spring celebration and was looking forward to Saturday evening. He had not been inside the buildings along the quay since he returned and was anxious to see what renovations had been finished. There were rumors that the workmen added a few features as they repaired the old buildings after the storm. He also looked forward to sharing the experience with Alius.

"The spring festival was fun," he said to his mother. "I've heard there are some improvements."

Elsie turned from the sink, where she was washing vegetables, "Well, it's supposed to be a surprise!"

Molly wandered in from the cold cellar with a basketful of flour, sugar, and honey. "I'm looking forward to the food!"

"You have a one track stomach!" giggled Megan.

"All the mothers bring their best dishes and I want to try them all!"

Megan puffed out her cheeks and held her blouse away from her body as if she was ready to explode. Everyone laughed together.

The fathers came in from the barn and George asked, "What would you think about a little demonstration of your diving suits? The elders have been wanting to see how they work and this might be a good opportunity to show everyone on the island some of the technology that we found on the Island of the Children."

Adrian and the girls cried, "Sure!" in unison.

"We could arrive by water!" said Megan.

"Oh, let's make it more interesting," giggled Molly. "Why don't we make it a real demonstration?"

John inquired, "Like what?"

"Well, we could retrieve something from deep water or from the little harbor on the other side of the mountain. Then they could see how fast we can move."

"That's a great idea. How about if we drop some *orbs* in the water and all of you can go retrieve them and bring them back to the festival?"

"I like that," said Adrian.

"Done, then," said George. "I'll call Ponte to see if he can come up with some *orbs* of different colors and you three can call your friends to see if they want to participate."

The children wandered off to the study to call the rest of the crew. Everyone wanted to show off what they learned on their journey.

Chapter 12

Sir Winston smiled, as he scanned the screens in the massive control room. "The connections are almost complete in the Atlantic Zone, Sire. There is one Black Crystal that is tied by an unusual vector to a Positive Crystal. We're only getting partial energy from that one but the technicians are working on it. In the meantime, we have enough power for a demonstration."

Zepallo turned to his assistant with a sinister smile, "I have just the thing! But, while we work on that, I want you to investigate that strange connection in person."

"I am at your service."

The Dark Lord settled back into his plan, "It's been a rather quiet hurricane season, let's create a storm that will be long remembered for its ferocity!"

"I will give the command!" replied Sir Winston, turning to a slender microphone. "We are about to create a hurricane. Focus the powers on the west coast of Africa five degrees north of the equator!"

The technicians scrambled to direct the energies of the dark vectors to form a small, almost insignificant, low-pressure system above the warm currents of the eastern Atlantic. Over the next few days, hot tropical water would evaporate from the surface of the ocean, rising to form massive clouds, and the wind would accelerate as it rushed to fill the void at the center of the infant storm.

Primed by an incessant influx of energy from the dark vectors and the earth's rotation, the storm would begin to rotate counter-clockwise, growing ever larger, as moisture evaporated from the super-heated surface of the ocean and moved skyward. As the storm matured, spiraling arms of thunderstorms fan out around the eye with wind speeds increasing to 200 miles per hour and waves cresting at more than fifty feet.

Northern equatorial currents drive tropical storms west and the powers were focused to clear out a high-pressure system perched over the Lesser Antilles. As the squall grew in strength, there would be no natural resistance to its movements.

Zepallo sat back in his chair and hissed, "Let this be their first warning!"

———————— ~~~ ————————

Adrian and the twins, Morgan, Kelly, Josh, and Ian were lined up on the dock in the harbor. Several hundred people crowded around the cove and the other children teased the group about their suits.

"You look like aliens," came one comment.

"Very stylish!"

"I bet you'll float like rubber duckies!"

Adrian spoke into his headset, "Don't worry about those fools, guys, we'll show them some new magic!"

His headset gurgled with giggles.

Ponte raised his hands for quiet. "We have placed seven *orbs* in the harbor on the north side of the mountain. Each of you will retrieve an *orb* and return it as quickly as possible. Are there any questions?"

The seven divers jumped into the cold, dark water. Air bubbles sheathed their suits and they zoomed off just beneath the surface where everyone could see their speed.

Morgan called out, "I'd forgotten how much fun this is! We need to do this more often!"

"I agree," said Josh.

"Let's show them what we can do!"

They flew over a rocky reef, scattering lobsters, shrimp, and crab. Schools of herring shimmered in the light cascading down from the surface, halibut swept up silt along the bottom, startled by the flock of speeding divers. Haddock and cod darted beneath a giant school of bluefish that glittered in the cold water. Each of the children smiled to themselves, captivated by the magic of this undersea world.

Within minutes, they flew into the second cove and Kelly was the first to spot an orange *orb* lying on the bottom, "I see one!"

"Go get it but join back up. We want to return together!"

Josh and Ian found two more *orbs* near the pilings under the docks. Adrian, Morgan, Molly, and Megan spread out and explored the bottom.

"Found one," called Molly.

"Me too," yelled Megan.

Morgan and Adrian dove to the deepest point in the harbor, where they found two *orbs* nestled together.

"We're done," called Morgan. "Let's go!"

Everyone merged into a small swarm and flashed through the bay. Spot and Dusty joined up as they cleared the jetties and a giant school of tuna, some weighing up to fifteen hundred pounds, shimmered like flickering silver *orbs* above them. Flying through the open ocean was exhilarating and Adrian thought, for a moment, about suggesting they not go back quite so directly but he knew the Professor was hoping to find support for expanding their facilities into the ocean.

As they veered into the cove, Kelly's voice crackled through the headsets, "I'm flying!"

Everyone turned to watch the tiny imp carving spirals through the water. A twisted stream of bubbles formed a trail behind her, effervescing like a glistening silver rope twirling through the black sea.

The seven divers reached the docks and surfaced together, thrusting the *orbs* above their heads. Elapsed time - five minutes.

Adrian looked up to find a broad smile on the Professor's face as he leaned, rather precariously, over the group in the water. "Well, done!" he laughed. The children scrambled up a ladder, unsealed their helmets, and lined up next to Ponte.

A roar went up, as he raised his hands and bellowed to the crowd, "If any of you were keeping track, you would note that these children took almost exactly five minutes to leave this harbor, swim around to the north end of the island, find and retrieve the *orbs*…which were scattered around the cove, and then return them to us. This is a small sample of what is possible using the technology that has been developed by our friends on the Island of the Children."

The crowd cheered and surrounded the divers, as they tried to make their way to the dock house, where they could change into regular clothes. The children, who teased them before the dive, now wanted to feel the fabric of their diving suits and ask questions about how fast they could go or how deep they could dive. The demonstration had been a resounding success.

The young divers entered the dining hall to find Simian and Sammy waiting at a long table at the center. Adrian gazed around the room, repainted in a soft gray and the ceiling imitated the one in the parlor at the observatory with stars and planets glowing against the dark background.

"This reminds me of the festivals that we have in Jamaica," said Sammy. "Everyone is joyful, there are flowers everywhere, and the food smells wonderful. I can't wait for dinner! My only complaint is that the music could be a little more…lively!" He pointed to the instruments playing without human assistance on the low stage at the far end of the room.

"Grown-up music," said Kelly. "I liked the music in Jamaica!"

"I wonder whether they take requests?" laughed Morgan.

"I think Ponte programmed the instruments," said Adrian. "It sounds like music he'd like."

"I'm bettin' you're right," said Molly. "Come on, let's go to the funhouse!"

Sammy looked confused, "Funhouse?"

"Oh, you'll like this," smiled Megan, grabbing his hand. "Hey, there's Alius, let's take her along!"

They gathered the little blond *seer* and wandered out through the fish shop, along the quay, and into the tackle shop in the next building.

Adrian watched Sammy's face, as they walked through the store. He gawked at the incredible variety of rods and reels, lures of every color, bobbers, hooks, lines of every length and thickness, and bait tanks, at the back, filled with glowing goldfish.

The little Jamaican peered into the first tank and smiled. "I don't think that anyone would catch much with these but they sure are pretty!"

Adrian laughed, "Come on, you'll enjoy this!"

As they stepped through the door at the back of the shop, they all stopped in wonder. The building had been almost completely demolished during the storm and the workmen from both sides of the island had pitched in to make it even better.

The giant colored eggs, floating a foot above the floor, had been repainted like voracious insects in wild colors and seemed to move a bit more swiftly, as they bumped and bounced amid peels of laughter from the children piloting them. The carousel had been rebuilt and the horses, butterflies, dragons, pandas, and unicorns refinished to appear more animated. New *orbs* had been installed overhead and a fog machine enfolded the riders in a cloud that glowed in an ever-changing rainbow of colors.

The roller coaster had been completely rebuilt and seemed to move faster than during the last festival. "Let's go!" screamed Molly.

They all piled into the new cars and found that the seats now wrapped around their shoulders, molding them in place. It was a good change because, when the coaster started up, it seemed to be going about twice as fast as their last ride.

The tiny train banged through a closed door at the top of the stairs and turned hard to the right, where a giant dragon leapt out with a mighty roar and a tongue of fire. The lions and tigers had been replaced with a herd of stampeding elephants and only a last minute swerve of the coaster saved the riders from being crushed by rampaging Goliaths.

They turned to the right into a darkened room that was suddenly vibrating to the rhythm of strobe lights that revealed pirates swinging gleaming swords at the riders as they passed. The children, who had visited the Island of the Children, all screamed with delight. Suddenly, they were taking dead aim at a blank wall. At the last possible moment, the wall exploded and they burst through the hole into fading sunlight. The cars rolled over backwards, crashed though a window on the other side of the building, only to fly through the structure, out another window, into a full twist through a door on the first floor, landing at the base of the stairs, where the ride started. Everyone was squealing with delight.

"Come on, let's go see what they've done with the tree house!" giggled Kelly, as she grabbed Alius' hand and skipped out the back door to the base of the giant oak tree.

Sammy stopped next the Adrian, as they looked up into the old oak. "This is the biggest tree I've ever seen. It's enormous!"

"The storm, that we told you about, broke several big branches and we were worried that it might not survive but you almost can't tell that it was damaged. See the disks at the base of the tree?"

Children were hopping onto the colored disks that floated up to deposit them on a platform, twenty feet above the ground. Sammy smiled and ran over to stand on a disk. In a moment, he was rising up into the foliage, waving at Adrian.

Adrian and Morgan waited for two disks to descend and floated up to Alius, Sammy, and Kelly on the platform. The slides had been repaired and children zoomed up and down and around the trunk of the old tree. Brandy came trotting up and brushed against Adrian's leg, "Nice swimming!"

Adrian leaned down to pet the red dog, "What is it about you and this tree? Dogs don't climb trees!"

"I didn't climb it. I rode a disk up to the platform and I do ride on the slides. Why shouldn't dogs climb trees?"

"I guess you have a point. In your case, nothing would surprise me!" laughed Adrian, hugging his friend.

The children showed Alius and Sammy how to jump on the slides and zoomed from one landing to the next until they reached the very top of the tree. A gap in the branches revealed a full moon rising above the horizon to the east and an orange sun setting behind the forest along the ridge to the west. The knot on the mountain, to the north, glowed a fiery red. They turned back to look down into the harbor where colored *orbs* had been installed around the entire perimeter. Little waves glistened with small explosions of red, blue, green, yellow, and purple. It was going to be a beautiful evening.

Morgan leaned over the railing, next to Adrian. "Are you alright? I sense that you're back in *seer* mode."

"Thanks for asking," smiled Adrian. "You're right. There's a new problem that Ponte and Nanchez are trying to figure out and Alius and I have been chained to the Books for what seems like days on end."

"I know you'll find an answer. I believe in you," said Morgan, as she snuggled closer and gave him a little hug.

Presently, the mothers appeared beneath the tree, calling the children to dinner. Brandy was the first to ride down on a disk. When he reached the ground, he looked up and grinned at Adrian. "Dinner is served!"

The children piled their plates with an incredible variety of treats. Sammy couldn't make up his mind. He took a bite of this and then a bite of that, closing his eyes to savor every new taste. "This is incredible. I want to try everything!"

"We'll have to pair you up with Molly," laughed Megan.

After dinner, other children gathered around the table to ask about the diving suits. Nanus, one of Alius' friends asked, "How fast can you go?"

Morgan smiled, "I don't honestly know our speed but it's faster than a boat on the surface."

"Do you get cold?"

"No, the suits and bubbles protect you. You don't even get wet," said Josh.

"I want to try it. Can we use your suits?"

"No, each suit is made to fit your exact proportions. Adrian's Mom learned how to make them from the tailors on the Island of the Children and his Dad learned about the communications gear and the system that creates the bubbles. They're hoping to convince the elders to let her begin making suits for everyone on the island," replied Ian.

"Did they really have a city under the sea?"

"Yeah, it's amazing. They have giant domes connected by glass tunnels. It's like being inside an upside-down fishbowl looking out at fish in the ocean...or, maybe, it's the other way 'round with them looking in at us! It's beautiful," added Molly.

"I hope they build one here!"

"I think they might consider it, now that they've seen what the suits allow us to do," said Adrian.

The music faded and the dancers applauded, as Ponte took the stage to announce, "We have a small surprise for everyone, if you would be kind enough to step outside."

The crowd slowly wandered out onto the quay and gathered on the docks around the little harbor. There were murmurs and quiet whispers, as the audience waited. Adrian noticed his father, George, Travis, Nanchez, and Mandor wander away from the crowd onto the arms of the jetties.

Ponte raised his hands for quiet and said, "Several months ago, we rescued my bride, Miss Ester, and, in the process, used up a surprise that I had been working on for your entertainment. Tonight, we would like to present a show in the stars!"

With that, the heavens exploded in colors, as fireworks rose from the wharf and filled the skies. The audience cheered each volley of red starbursts, golden fountains, brilliant flares from Ponte's flashpans, blue streamers, and purple flowers. The show went on for almost half an hour before the grand finale filled the skies with glittering explosions and the jetties erupted in fountains of golden sparks. The crowd loved it.

Adrian noticed Sammy staring intently across the cove and followed his gaze to Simian, who was standing with Elsie, Sara, and John. His eyes were closed and the expression on his face was anxious rather than joyous.

The two boys pushed through the crowds along the docks and Sammy whispered to Simian. "Are you alright?"

"Yes, yes…I felt a vibration through the vectors and I see that there is a disturbance in our home. A hurricane is approaching. We must go back to help our people."

Sammy whispered in Adrian's ear. "If he must go, then I must go with him."

Adrian patted his friend on the shoulder. "Can he transport the two of you that far?"

"I don't know. He's never tried to travel that distance."

Simian turned and pressed through the throng to Ponte, who was chatting with Jofre. He whispered something to the Professor who turned with a troubled look on his face. They spoke for a few moments and Simian motioned for Sammy. He said, "We will be leaving tonight."

Sammy leaned over to Adrian and whispered above the noise of the crowd, "We're leaving tonight."

"I'm sorry. I hope you can come right back. There is much more for each of you to learn."

"I know and I don't want to leave but Simian is right, the reason that we are here is to learn how to help our people. If there is a hurricane headed for Jamaica, then we must do what we can."

Adrian stared at the stars that filled the sky, "I wonder…?"

"You wonder what?"

"We told you about the storm that the *Others* created here on Morgan's Knot. I wonder whether the people who are working with the dark vectors could create a giant storm?"

"I don't know," replied Sammy. "The only difference is that this one is much bigger."

"We'll have to ask the Professor about this and it's just one more reason why you need to come back. We need your help to discover what's happening with the Black Crystals and what we can do to stop them."

Two hours later, the *seers* gathered with Sammy, Ponte, Ester, Jofre, Nanchez, George, and Travis, in the Professor's parlor.

Simian stood in front of the embers of a desperately dim fire, "There is a hurricane headed for our homeland. We must return there to help with preparations."

Jofre inquired, "How do you know this?"

"I felt a disturbance in the vectors. The connection between the Green Crystal in Jamaica and the Golden Crystal of Morgan's Knot is very strong."

Nanchez asked, "Have you ever tried to travel that far?"

"No, but I'm sure that we will be alright. The technique that we've been teaching to Adrian and Alius does not depend on distance but rather the strength of the vector connection between the two points."

"Is there anything that we can do to help you?" asked George.

"Unless you can divert the storm, no," replied Simian. "The things that we must do are very human, protecting the lives and property of our family and our people. This does not involve the magic of the Crystals but the magic of the human heart."

Everyone nodded.

Ester chimed in, "You must return to us. There's much for each of you to learn and even more that we might learn from you."

"We will come back when the storm has passed," smiled Simian. "I want to thank all of you for your hospitality and your friendship. I think that we've both learned to respect The Balance and this way of life."

Everyone shook hands or hugged the two men and then stood in a circle.

Simian smiled, "We'll see you soon." He placed his hand on Sammy's shoulder, closed his eyes, and, in a flash, vanished.

"I wonder how long it will take them to get there," wondered Sara.

"It wouldn't surprise me if they weren't there already," replied Nanchez.

Adrian leaned over to the Professor and said, "If the *Others* could produce the storm here on Morgan's Knot, could the people who are working with the Black Crystals create a giant storm?"

The Professor stared at the young man for a moment, "I don't see why not. Could this be a demonstration?"

Adrian motioned to Alius to follow him into the dining room. They sat at the table and opened the books. Adrian asked, "Is the hurricane that is heading for Jamaica a natural storm or was it created by humans?"

The grown-ups gathered around the table in silence.

The Books responded, "It is not natural."

"Are the people who are connecting the dark vectors responsible for the storm?"

Alius looked up at Adrian, "The Silver Book says, 'Yes'."

The two *seers* turned to Ponte and Nanchez, who stared back in silence. Finally, Ponte almost whispered, "You two are excused from classes next week. You'll be busy here."

Chapter 13

Captain Max Lee struggled to guide the old C-130 through the furious storm. Winds of 150 miles per hour tossed the aircraft up and down like a child's glider and hail, pelting the fuselage, rattled like machine gun rounds.

They entered the edge of the hurricane from the west, as the center chugged towards the Caribbean Sea to the south of the Lesser Antilles. The cloud mass was over one thousand miles across and the leading arms stretched from the northeastern coast of South America to Puerto Rico and the Dominican Republic. John Adams, a meteorologist, tapped his instruments and stared at the barometer. "The pressure's dropping like a rock. This one's gonna to be a monster."

"Roger that," replied the co-pilot.

These men were professionals. They had flown into many storms over the years but they all knew that this could be the Big One, a vicious storm capable of shredding this specially reinforced aircraft. Each man understood that their lives depended on their training and equipment. If the plane went down, there could be no rescue.

"Wall of the eye coming up," called the navigator.

"Let's hope we make it!" exclaimed co-pilot Cameron.

Moments later, the plane was tossed up a thousand feet by a violent upsurge and popped out of the clouds into the eye of the storm. The sky cleared, sunlight poured down into the huge column, and the air was relatively calm. Trapped and exhausted seagulls coasted on thermals below and the airplane was dwarfed by giant rotating wall-clouds that extended for thousands of feet above and below the plane.

They flew in a long slow spiral around the inside of the storm and determined that the core was less than twenty miles across. The pressure within the tight, well-defined eye matched the record for the lowest ever recorded. When the mass of the storm hit land, brutal winds, gigantic surf, and torrential flooding would create devastation for anyone or anything in its path.

The crew radioed their information back to the Storm Center in Miami and turned north, into the thickest arm of the storm. Whoever manned the next flight into the tempest would find the hurricane even more violent, as it extracted energy from the warm waters of the Caribbean.

With no major weather masses to obstruct its course, the storm could continue west into the Yucatan, or turn slightly to the north into the Gulf of Mexico, or make a right turn across Cuba and bump along the eastern coast of the United States. At this point, the experts in Miami could not predict the exact tract or where the storm might reach landfall.

Chapter 14

Adrian and Alius were hunched over the Books on the dining room table, suffering through a torrent of technical questions about the fluctuations in the current being produced by the Black Crystal.

Adrian sat back in his chair and sighed with frustration. "We know what's happening but we don't know how it's being done. We know who's directing this but we don't know where he is and, even more important, we don't know why. We suspect that whoever is connecting the Black Crystals is controlling the hurricane that could strike Jamaica as a demonstration of their power. What could they do if they connected all the Crystals in the world into a complete network?"

Everyone stared for a moment before Ester made that sound in her throat and said, "I think you should ask the last question first. What would happen if all of the Black Crystals were connected together?"

Alius glanced at Adrian, then asked, "What will happen when all of the Black Crystals are connected together?"

The figures rushed around the pages for what seemed a very long time. Finally, they formed a globe shrouded in a black fog.

There was total silence in the room, which was shattered by a loud alarm. Ponte and Ester jumped from their chairs in panic. Adrian and Alius covered their ears and Nanchez looked slightly bewildered.

"We have visitors!" exclaimed Ponte, as he mashed a button on a console in the parlor to silence the warning. "Everyone to the village!"

The group scrambled outside and jumped into the Professor's crazy trolley and Nanchez' large truck. They raced along the path, hauling a huge plume of dust in their wake.

By the time they reached the village, people were scrambling around on the docks carting supplies from storage sheds into the shops. Adrian could hear Elsie shrieking at the men who were carrying frozen fish for display in the cases in the fishmonger's shop and, the girls were right, her shrill voice really did sound like the fishmonger's wife!

John ran up to Adrian and Alius and handed them two fishing rods. "Go sit on the dock and fish."

The *seers* took the poles and sat down on the edge of the dock. They tied sinkers onto the end of their lines and hooked bobbers, allowing a few feet of line to dangle in the water.

Molly and Megan joined Josh and Ian, kicking a ball around, and Ponte sat on a stool with a tattered newspaper in his lap, on the far side of the cove, watching Morgan blowing bubbles with Kelly. He looked the perfect grandfather.

Presently, a huge luxury yacht idled into the harbor. It was so large it could barely make the turn to pull up next to the only open dock. Aside from a few chrome and white accents, the ship was completely black. The captain, dressed in a formal white uniform, stepped through a door on the bridge. "Ahoy! Would you catch our lines?"

John and Travis caught ropes thrown from bow and stern by impeccably outfitted sailors and tied them off to cleats. George wandered over to the side of the ship, "Greetings!"

"I'm afraid I don't find your island on our charts. Does this island have a name?"

"Aye, it's called Morgan's Knot. It's so small, the mapmakers must have overlooked us!"

"May we disembark?"

"Certainly!"

The captain disappeared inside the ship and reappeared with a tall, slender gentleman, dressed in an expensive black silk suit, accented by a red tie, perfectly quaffed silver hair escaping beneath a bowler sitting squarely on his head, and a sculpted goatee. He carried a carved walking stick with a black crystalline knob on the end that seemed more style than necessity. He offered his arm to a stunningly beautiful Chinese woman in a flowing blue suit that appeared to be made of the same delicate fabric that Simian sold to Sara and Morgan in Jamaica.

The captain, the tall man, and the Chinese woman slowly made their way down the gangplank to the dock. Ponte rose, gathered the girls, and strolled along the quay to the yacht. The other children moved closer to ogle the visitors and their beautiful ship.

Adrian stared at the tall man in the bowler hat. A shiver ran down his spine, much like the feeling he had when he first looked at the mountain, and he sensed there was more to this accidental visitor than he would reveal.

The Captain said, "Allow me to introduce Sir Winston Dodd and his companion, Madame Ming. I am Captain Foster and this," he said, gesturing to the yacht, "is the Black Diamond."

"Nice to meet you," said George, "I'm George and this is Travis and John." Sara stepped out the small crowd gathered to inspect the ship. "Oh, and John's wife, Sara."

"How can we help you?"

"Well, we'd love to tour your shops," said the tall man. "Tell me, is there property for sale on this island. I'm always looking for vacation homes in special places. This is certainly a beautiful island."

"You're welcome to tour the shops but I'm afraid that, for the most part, we carry only necessities. I'm sure the shopping is much better on the larger islands."

"I'm sure you're right but they don't have the charm of this little village and beautiful women live to shop," smiled the tall man, as he took Madame Ming's arm. "Shall we go?"

John led the guests along the docks and they gazed in the windows of the fishmonger's shop, the tackle shop, and the little grocery. The Chinese woman gently gripped Sir Winston's arm and floated along the quay on tiny graceful steps. They stopped to admire embroidered children's dresses in the window of the seamstress shop.

"Oh, may I look at these little dresses?" asked Madame Ming. "My niece's first birthday is coming up."

"Certainly, my dear," said the tall man, "I'll wait for you here."

The Englishman held the door and she wandered into the shop. Mrs. Stevens greeted her and showed her several little gowns.

Sir Winston turned to George, "You didn't answer my question. Are there any properties for sale on the island?"

"No, I'm afraid there aren't. All of the homes have been owned by the same families for generations."

"That's too bad. This seems an exceptional sanctuary from the hustle and bustle."

George smiled, "It is very beautiful but I'm afraid that it isn't terribly exciting. We're mostly farmers and fishermen and there isn't much nightlife, other than a bunch of old timers getting together to tell tall tales and outright lies in our little tavern on occasion."

"At my age, my friend, I'm well past the need or the desire to seek out the temptations of the night," laughed Sir Winston. "Although, when I was younger...!"

George laughed with the tall man, as they strolled past the little pub and the apothecary before returning to the seamstress's shop. Madame Ming was just coming out with a white box, tied with silver ribbons.

"You found something for your niece?" asked the tall man.

"Oh, yes. It's lovely," replied the Chinese woman. "The seamstress' work is magnificent."

Sir Winston turned to George, "Tell me, what is the most special thing about this island?"

George lifted his weathered hat to brush his hair back, grinning, "The people of course."

"Special people make a special place, I am envious of all that you have here."

The group sauntered back to the gangplank, where a small herd of children were still gathered alongside the beautiful ship, and the tall man happened to brush Adrian's shoulder as he passed. Adrian felt that tingling he felt when he first shook hands with Simian. He looked up at the tall man and realized that he sensed it too. Adrian smiled bashfully.

The tall man turned to George without acknowledging Adrian, "I thank you for you time. Perhaps we will meet again."

"You have a safe journey," smiled George, as he shook the man's hand. Madame Ming bowed gracefully and scaled the gangplank to the deck of the black ship. The lines were cast off and the yacht motored slowly out of the cove.

Everyone waited until it turned past the end of jetty before erupting in laughter. "I think we fooled another one!" laughed Travis.

"I'm not so sure," replied George. "I've a strange feeling about that one."

Adrian walked up to his uncle, "He might not be a *seer* but he is involved with the powers. I felt a little shock when he passed by."

Everyone turned to listen. "I get these feelings about people and things that are connected to the Crystals. That man is connected," said Adrian to everyone and no one.

"Tell you what," said the Professor, "you children go put on your diving suits while I fetch a tracking crystal from the trolley. Let's see where they're headed."

The children scrambled off to Travis' dock-house and changed into their diving suits. By the time they returned, Ponte was waiting with a shimmering blue crystal in a magnetic mount.

"Just touch it to the hull of the ship and it'll stick. Stay away from the propellers and don't get too near their sonar gear or they might pick up the interference," instructed the Professor. "And come right back when you're finished!"

Adrian took the Crystal and inserted it in the pouch on the arm of his suit. All of the children jumped into the water and, as the bubbles sparkled around them, zoomed off through the gap between the jetties.

They dove deep and followed the sound of the giant yacht's engines. Within minutes, the swarm of children coasted along directly beneath the hull of the ship. Adrian noticed that there were no fish around and said, "You guys stay here and I'll go stick this on the hull."

He swam almost straight up and attached the blue crystal to the side of a shallow keel running from bow to stern. It stuck on the first try. Adrian felt a deep, electric vibration when he touched the hull of the yacht. He pulled his hand away and stared at the fingertips of his gloved hand. The tingling disappeared but, after weeks on the Jasmine, he knew that the vibration was different from that produced by a ship's engines. He dove to join his friends and they zoomed off along the bottom into a long slow curve into the harbor.

By the time the children surfaced in the cove, most of the crowd had dispersed. Ponte rose from his little stool, as the divers climbed a ladder to the dock.

"Mission accomplished," crowed Kelly, pulled her headpiece off to shake out her blond hair.

"Well done!"

Adrian released his helmet, "There's more to that yacht than we realized. I felt another shock, as I attached the blue crystal. They must be running some sort of scanning device. I wonder whether they're checking out the powers of the Crystals?"

"That may be," replied the Professor. "Nanchez has already gone back to check our instruments. We'll track them to see where they go and what they're up to."

As the children moved off to the dock-house to change, Ponte wandered over to George and Travis. The old shipmaster looked concerned, "What do you make of it?"

George said, "I'm not sure but Adrian said that he felt a shock, when Sir Winston brushed past him, and I tend to put a great deal of faith into his hunches. If you ask me, I'd say they were here to survey the island."

Alius had been sitting on the edge of the dock, watching the other children as they left and then returned from their mission. She stood up and walked over to the adults. "I think they're involved with Zepallo. How many pairs of Crystals are bound together to produce the magic that we enjoy on this island or on The Island of the Children?"

Ponte smiled, "That's a question we should ask the Books. It's something that we've never explored and I've often wondered how many other places there are on this planet that are using the powers. Not only how many but what are they doing with them? Even on Morgan's Knot, the North and the South were using them in different ways and both sides managed to find secrets the other missed. Add to that calculation the wonders that we found on the Island of the Children and I must conclude that there are probably places where the people have found even more fantastic properties that we have yet to discover."

The other children wandered out of the dock-house and around the cove to join Alius and the adults. Morgan walked next to Adrian, "Is this part of the problem that you were talking about?"

"Yes, I'm sure these people are a part of it," said Adrian quietly.

"This is different from the other challenges you've faced," whispered Morgan.

"This one's scarier than anything we've had to deal with yet."

"Do you still want to go back to being that boy who arrived here a few months ago?"

Adrian blushed, "No, now I have to go forward. There is no other choice."

"I knew you'd say that," smiled Morgan, as she squeezed his hand. "You can't change the person that you are in your heart."

Alius was waiting for them and moaned, "I want to learn to dive with you!"

Adrian smiled, "Actually, my Mom and Mandor were talking at the festival, the other night, and I overheard Mandor saying that there was a scanner in the medical lab in the mountain that could be used to provide patterns for the diving suits. My mother is anxious to begin making them."

"Oh, I hope so! I can't wait!"

Ponte interrupted, "I think that your diving instruction will have to wait a little longer. Would you two be kind enough to come back to the observatory for a few more questions?"

"Of course," said Alius, scrunching up her face at Adrian, who burst out laughing.

Chapter 15

Ester, Ponte, Alius, and Adrian started through the dining room as the elevator doors parted and Nanchez' enormous frame erupted from the tiny car. "I've piped the signal up to your *messenger*. We should be able to track them from the parlor."

"Wonderful," said Ponte, as he turned to the *orb* and commanded, "Data!"

The *messenger* glowed and a map of the island appeared before the screen. The blue crystal, still snug on the hull of the Black Dragon, appeared as a pulsating sapphire, moving slowly around the island.

The dot slowed to idle speed outside the *Other's* little harbor, veered around the craggy black mountain at the north end of the island, and then proceeded south along the rocky west coast.

"I wonder," mused Ponte.

Everyone turned, waiting for the rest of his thought.

"If they are aware of the Crystals, I wonder whether they're scanning the island?"

Nanchez smiled, "We used to scan you before...I think I could focus our scanner on the yacht. Actually, I could do it by remote from your workshop."

Everyone trooped to the elevator and descended to the white room, where the Golden Crystal turned smoothly on its axis, painting intense golden glimmers streaking around the curving contours of the cavern. They turned down a passage past several open alcoves and entered the workroom, passing a line of humming machines on the right. The Keepers rushed to the workbench against the left wall.

Ponte made several connections and stepped aside to allow Nanchez to dial in the codes that would allow remote control of the scanner in the mountain.

One of the *messengers* on the bench displayed the movement of the blue dot. A second sprang to life, showing a slightly different perspective, presenting the yacht as a yellow box on a blue background. As Nanchez entered more data, a red cone appeared, spreading from the yellow shape towards the island. It was aimed directly at the observatory.

Everyone watched in silence. The ship drifted to the bottom of the screen, as she moved south, but the red cone, displaying their scanner, remained directed at the Golden Crystal.

"Well, I think we've answered that question," commented Ester quietly.

"Let's continue to monitor them. I'll be curious to see where the Black Dragon goes next," pondered Ponte. "Pipe this upstairs and we can keep an eye on them, while we work with the Books."

Everyone crammed into the small elevator and emerged into the dining room. Adrian and Alius sat down at the table, while Ponte and Nanchez went into the living room to adjust the *messenger.*

Tic was sitting on the back of the sofa. Every hair on his body was standing on end and his eyes glistened like glossy black saucers. He wrapped his paws over his ears, screeching, "What are you working on? That sound is driving me crazy!"

Ponte and Nanchez looked at each other. "It must be their scanner!"

Nanchez reached a huge hand and wrapped Tic in his arms. "I'm sorry, kitty. The bad men are making that noise. Hopefully, they'll go away soon."

Before they could return to the dining room, Alius asked the Book of Knowledge, "How many pairs of Crystals are there in the world?"

"Fifty-seven."

"Are there people working with other pairs of Crystals?"

Adrian smiled, as he watched the figures roam around the page. "Yes."

"How many are there?" asked Adrian.

"Thirty-three."

"Where are they?"

The figures seemed to stop for a moment and then formed a diamond shape. It was Gold. Adrian sighed. He knew that, sooner or later, they would reach a point that would leave no other option but to enter the Crystal again. Although he was awed and fascinated by the interaction with the Golden Gem, he was anxious about the energy draining from his body, as if his very essence might flicker and fade like the flame on a candle in the wind, and his deference to those powers bordered on fear.

Nanchez and Ponte returned, as Alius asked, "Are there other pairs vectored together?"

"A few."

"Are the connections dependent on the nodes?"

"Yes."

"Are the nodes tied together?"

"No."

The two *seers* sat back in their chairs. Adrian said, "Okay, now we know there are thirty-three other places on the planet where people are working with the Crystals. We know about Morgan's Knot and the Island of the Children and Jamaica. We might assume that more than one of those thirty-three is being used by Zepallo and his people. I wonder where the rest of the pairs are and what those people have found?"

"You haven't found an answer in the Books?" asked Nanchez.

"No. The Books don't tell us where the pairs are or, for that matter, where the nodes are. It's as if we aren't allowed to explore beyond a certain limit, as if we're locked out."

Alius interrupted, "We know the vectors are dependent on the nodes and there are seven places where the vectors from the other Crystals connect to the nodes. We also know that the nodes are not directly linked to each other and that the Black Crystals must be connected individually."

"Well, that would explain our visitors," mused Ester. "They were trying to find out why they can't pull more power out of our Black Crystal."

Ponte smiled, "That should have been obvious to all of us. Thank you for pointing it out."

Nanchez turned to check the *messenger*. "They've come back around to the north side of the island. They're moving very slowly."

The yellow shape was barely crawling across the screen but the red cone of their scanner swept back and forth between the mountain and the observatory.

Ponte broke the silence, as everyone followed the yellow smudge on the screen. "Several things seem more important now than they did when we first learned them. The first is that the Golden Crystals are more powerful than the Black Crystals. Second, all of the Golden Crystals could be connected together through the nodes, although we don't know exactly how to do that or even where. And third, the connection that we made between our two Crystals is causing a problem for Sir Winston and Zepallo."

Everyone considered his thoughts for a moment before Adrian said, "The answers that we're seeking can't be found in the Books."

Ponte stared at the young *seer* for a moment. "I know what you're suggesting, and entering the Crystal might be the only answer, but I would suggest that we all think about what we've learned. When we know the right questions to ask, then we might consider such a step."

The *seers* closed the Books and rose from the table. Adrian walked over to the purple sofa to pet Tic. "Is the sound still bothering you?"

"It's still there but not as intense as it was earlier," said Tic, covering his ears with his paws.

Adrian looked at the *messenger*. The black ship was moving off to the east and the cone had broadened to include the entire island. "They're looking at the vector system over the whole island!"

Everyone gathered around the *messenger* to watch as it slowly moved away. The red cone disappeared from the screen, as the yellow spot continued east. Tic lifted his paws from his ears, "Ah, that's better."

The yellow shape and the blue dot stopped moving. Suddenly another shape appeared on the screen next to the yellow shape. This one was a very dim shade of orange. After a few minutes, the second blip disappeared.

"What was that?" asked Alius.

Ponte rubbed his chin for a moment, "My dear, that was a submarine. Our friend, Sir Winston, just changed ships!"

"Rats!" exclaimed Nanchez. "The tracking crystal would provide a signal we could follow for hundreds of miles but it won't do us any good if he's on another ship!"

"Right you are, my friend. He's gone," smiled the Professor. "We'll just have to find another way to locate their Ice Island but let's track the Black Diamond anyway, might give us another clue."

Adrian picked up the cat and held him in his arms. He turned to Ester, "Could I borrow Tic for a while?"

"Certainly, but what are you going to do?"

"Well, I was just thinking about how Simian takes Sammy, when he travels along the vectors, and I was wondering whether I could do the same thing."

Ester tut-tutted and looked concerned, "You must bring him back safe and sound!"

"Oh, I will. I promise," said Adrian, stroking Tic's fur. "Would you like to spend some time at the House of the Four Seasons and I'll bring you back later?"

Tic purred, "Sure. I'd like to run down to the Keelty's to see Brandy anyway."

Nanchez and Alius left the observatory and Adrian said good-bye to the Professor and Ester. He held Tic very close, closed his eyes, and concentrated on the vegetable garden. A moment later, he was gone.

Chapter 16

Sir Winston stood behind Madame Ming, who was scanning the data at a sleek console in a cabin on The Black Dragon. The tall man admired his associate, who was capable of transforming from demure and stunningly beautiful radiance into a lethal assassin with a black belt in karate, and she was their most proficient technician.

"This is interesting," said Madame Ming. "The Black Crystal is located in the mountain and the Positive Crystal is buried beneath the plain that flows to the south just east of the ridgeline. They've installed a connecting vector to harness the power from both Crystals. Our systems can pull partial power from the Black Crystal but we have no way to override the link they've installed."

"Are you saying that we can not gain control of the Black Crystal?"

"That is correct, although we are pulling some energy into our system," said the Chinese woman. "We're drawing enough power from all of the other Crystals but I would guess that we will run into this problem in other places, where the power of the Crystals is being harnessed by local Keepers. I'll run some simulations when we get back to base to see whether we can overcome this problem once we've joined all of the other Crystals."

"Once we've connected all of the rest of the Black Crystals in the world, it might not make any difference. We will have control. I'll report to Lord Zepallo."

Madame Ming checked her scanner, "The sub is approaching. Send your message. Our assignment is fulfilled."

Sir Winston sat down at the workstation and flipped on the *messenger*. He entered a secret code and waited. Presently, Zepallo's face appeared, "I take it that you have completed your mission, Sir Winston."

"That is correct. Our initial finding is that they have installed an unusual vector, between the Black and White Crystals, which is limiting the amount of power that can be drawn from the Black Crystal. Madame Ming has forwarded the data and is testing for a way around the link. We do not think that it will impair our plans."

Zepallo did not look happy. "And what of the residents?"

"I recorded our entire visit on the crystal in my cane but I had a chance encounter with a bashful young man and I am absolutely sure that he is a *seer*. From the distribution of vectors across the island, it seems obvious that they are using The Powers. Without further investigation, we have no way of knowing their level of sophistication but I have no reason to believe that they have any reason to suspect our plans."

"This young man could be a problem."

"He is only a boy," said Sir Winston.

"We were boys once and young boys are cursed with curiosity. They snoop in places where they have no business looking. I am not comfortable with your findings."

"All the more reason to move ahead quickly. How is our weather phenomenon developing?"

"It is progressing as planned. The storm is sailing to the west and will hit the first islands in a few days. At the moment, it is a category 4. They have named it Francisco."

"That is wonderful. Our transportation has arrived. We will see you in about eight hours."

"Have a safe journey," said Zepallo. There was no smile on his face, as the glow of the *messenger* faded.

Sir Winston shivered. He had the misfortune of witnessing the Dark Lord's wrath at a lieutenant who failed to fulfill a command. Avoiding the lash of his master's rage was paramount to maintaining his position and his survival.

Chapter 17

Adrian, Brandy, and the girls were out in the yard playing with a crazyball, when George called Adrian to answer a call. He ran into the house and followed his uncle to the study. The Professor's face hovered in front of the *messenger*.

"Good evening, my boy. How are you?"

"I'm fine. What can I do for you?"

"Well, I've been working with Nanchez on our little problem. We think that we've reached a point where we need answers that only you can provide. Could you come by in the morning?"

Adrian stared at the screen. He knew exactly what Ponte was suggesting and hesitated, "I'll be there after breakfast."

"Get a good night's sleep!" Ponte's image faded.

The following morning, Adrian finished his breakfast, kissed his mother, and hugged his father. "I have to go to the observatory. The Professor needs more information."

"You be careful," said Sara, as she brushed blond curls out of his eyes. "I'll give you a haircut this afternoon."

Adrian avoided the bit about his upcoming excursion, knowing they would worry and there was little they could do to help. He grabbed Tic, walked outside, and said, "Are you ready to go home?"

Tic purred, "Sure. This is fun!" He looked up into the young *seer's* blue eyes, "There is one more thing. You've realized that understanding the powers is demanding."

"I think I'm beginning to understand the weight of your warning," replied Adrian.

"The more you learn, the heavier the responsibility. You do realize that this puzzle, you're trying to solve, will reach a flash point and you'll be asked to go beyond anything you've been asked to do before?"

"I know but I've little choice, other than following this invisible, inevitable, and terrifying pathway...wherever it leads."

"I don't think we'll be able to help you on this one but I wish we could."

"I know," replied Adrian. He wrapped Tic inside his jacket, concentrated on the parlor at the observatory, and disappeared.

A moment later, he was standing in the living room at the Professor's house. Nanchez, Alius, Ponte, and Ester were all gathered around the old oak table in the dining room. Alius was concentrating on the Book of Knowledge.

"Ah, my boy, it's good to see you," smiled the Professor.

"As I promised," said Adrian, settling Tic on the back of the sofa.

"Let's review. We must assume that the hurricane bearing down on Jamaica, Francisco isn't it, is being driven by the power of the Black Crystals. I spoke with Dadeus last night and he's been running tests on the vectors and agrees that the storm is anything but natural."

"We know that the powers of the Positive Crystals are stronger than those produced by the Black Gems but if all of the Dark Crystals are chained together, their power will certainly be immense."

"The questions that need answers seem to be...whether the nodes can be hooked together, whether that energy could be focused to neutralize the power being produced through the dark vectors, and whether there is a way to stop Zepallo and his associates."

Adrian grinned, "Basically, can we short circuit their operation?"

"That's it!" said Nanchez.

Alius looked up at her friend, "Are you sure you're up to doing this again?"

"There are only two *seers* on the island and I have the experience."

"Then let us proceed," said Ponte quietly.

The elevator plunged down to the chamber where the Golden Crystal was spinning a foot above the floor scattering a blinding glow of mesmerizing golden radiance.

Adrian shielded his eyes and walked over to brush the gold dust from the smooth surface beneath the Crystal. He withdrew the golden key from his pocket and inserted it into the slot. A booming voice asked, "Who wishes to enter?"

"I am Adrian. I am a *seer!*"

He turned for a last look at the group and noticed Alius holding her hands over her ears. She heard the voice, although Adrian was sure that no one else could.

The speed of the Crystal's rotation increased and a hazy dark shadow appeared. When it was large enough, he stepped through the notch to land on the small smooth crystal, surrounded by the familiar figures, which were marching randomly around the interior. The globe appeared, rotating slowly, and the landmasses spread apart to form the continents. Glowing dots displayed the locations of the Crystals across the globe and a few disappeared as it turned.

Adrian tried to remember where all the dots were located but there were too many. Finally, the booming voice asked, "How can We help you?"

Adrian took a deep breath and tried to focus on the questions that needed to be asked. He could feel the energy draining down through spongy legs while his body wobbled like a spinning top about to topple from the axis of the whirling crystal.

"There is an evil man who is trying to connect the energies of all of the Black Crystals. From our readings in the Texts, we believe that those connections must be made individually. We have also learned that the Positive Crystals are connected through a series of seven nodes and we interpret the information that we found to mean that the Positive Crystals are more powerful than the negative."

"We have felt the disruption and, after our previous conversations, you must know that if the vectors of the Black Crystals are all connected into one circuit, it will doom the balance of the Powers."

"If all of the Positive Crystals were hooked together, would that generate sufficient power to overcome the energies of the Black Crystals?"

"Yes."

"How would that be accomplished?"

"You would need seven ruby Crystals. The gems must be deposited in each of the node Crystals by a *seer*."

"How would they be inserted?"

A small, gleaming circle appeared to his left, surrounded by concentric colored rings pulsing from the outside into infinity. Adrian noticed that the ring in the middle was approximately the same size as the mounts for the balancing crystals on the mountain and in the cave on La Isla de los Ninas.

The deep voice rumbled around him, "The Positive Crystals are grouped around seven Nodes. You have enhanced the vectors from this island to the Island of the Children and from the Black Crystal to the Golden Crystal, providing a link between the stones."

"Using the ruby Crystals to bond the nodes, every Positive Crystal in the world will become directly interconnected. The vectors will be permanently fixed to each other."

Adrian considered the information for a moment. He felt his energy waning. "Is there a negative effect of joining all the nodes?"

"If the vectors of each system were united, there would be a complete balance. The Positive would dominate the Negative and it would be possible to pulse power from the White to the Black, defusing the potential of the dark vectors."

"There is a Ruby Crystal on la Isle de los Ninas."

"That is an ideal source."

"How would I find the nodes?"

"Collect the seven ruby gems and use the vectors to move to your target Crystals. We have felt you moving across the vectors on the island. It is a similar experience, although far more dangerous."

"Why is it more dangerous?"

"Because, instead of moving from one point to another on a single vector, moving from one node to another requires you to bounce through a snarl of links, from one Crystal to another, until you reach your destination."

"Could other *seers* help?"

"It would be useful if they were familiar with transporting themselves through the vectors…but, yes, your fellow *seers* could assist in this task."

"Where are the nodes?"

Adrian could almost feel a sly grin radiating from inside the Crystal. *"Does this power have a sense of humor?"*

"The nodes are the most powerful Crystals on the planet. At one time, there were thirteen and all of the positive vectors flowed across the planet. Where man stumbled across them, spiritual centers evolved, just as more modest communities, like this one, have flourished using the powers of the remaining Crystals. In five of those six cases, man became greedy for the powers and the Crystals and the cultures withered into history. The rest have remained hidden, although the powers affected events that emanated from those places and the buildings that man erected on those sites."

"So you're saying that empires in places like Atlantis, Babylon, and Athens were built on sites where the nodes existed?"

"Yes."

"What about the odd one?"

"The sixth node was in Himalayas and it disappeared, not because the people were greedy for power but simply because the continents shifted and it was crushed. Can you name the remaining seven?"

Adrian pondered the question, straining to recall his geography classes, and flashed on the mural on the wall of the chamber under the pyramid on the Island of the Children. "I would guess St. Peter's Cathedral in Rome, The Forbidden City in Beijing, The Holy Mount in Jerusalem, someplace in Washington, Egypt, someplace in the Andes, and, perhaps, Stonehenge."

"Well, you are remarkably correct in naming Rome, Peking, Jerusalem, and Stonehenge. There is one under the Lincoln Memorial in Washington, D.C., another at the headwaters of the Amazon River in the mountains of eastern Peru, and one beneath the Sphinx in Egypt. The Egyptians didn't draw too much power from their Crystals. Their civilization was destroyed because they betrayed their beliefs to those of invading cultures. They stopped believing in The Balance."

Adrian could barely stand, "I will find the seven Ruby Crystals and seek the help of two other *seers*."

He felt that smile again, "Your time is short."

"Thank you," said the young *seer*, as the figures resumed their march around the interior of the Crystal. The dark hole appeared to his right and he stepped into the blinding light of the white room outside.

Ponte, Nanchez, Ester, and Alius were all standing immediately under the opening and caught him, as he collapsed into their arms.

Chapter 18

Adrian awoke to his mother wiping his face with a cool damp cloth. The concern in her eyes made him feel guilty for not telling her of his plans.

"I should be so mad at you! Why didn't you tell us what you were going to do?"

"I didn't want you to worry."

"When you didn't show up for lunch, I called Ester and found out what happened. She explained what you've been working on, and I understand why you entered the Crystal, but the next time I want to know ahead of time!"

"Yes, Mam."

"How are you feeling?"

"Weak…but…I know how to stop Zepallo!" he said, struggling to sit up. His head was pounding and his arms and legs felt heavy and slow. "We need seven Ruby Crystals."

Ponte was seated in the old wingchair in front of the smoldering fireplace, "I only have two. They are very rare."

"There are plenty on the Island of the Children," sighed Adrian, cradling his head in his hands.

"We are here and they are there," said Ester.

"I could move through the vectors to collect them."

"You've not been fully trained and you've only been moving around the island. We don't even know if Simian and Sammy made it back to Jamaica," warned Nanchez.

"I know I can do it," said Adrian. "But I'll need help. I want to take Alius with me. Three or four *seers* can work faster than I could alone."

Everyone turned to Alius. Her mouth was agape and a glint in her eyes betrayed her anxiety. "I've only bounced around the island a little bit," she said anxiously, "but I'll do whatever we need to do to stop Zepallo."

The two *seers* stared at each other. Adrian felt Alius drawing strength from his resolve and sensed the tension growing in the adults but he could not divert his eyes from her gaze. He waited until he was sure that they were sharing the same thought. It was almost like Simian's description of seeing along the vectors, except he was feeling inside another human being.

Alius smiled. It was settled.

Adrian turned to the Professor. "We'll go together to collect the ruby Crystals. We'll have to teach Raffe how to travel along the paths in a hurry and then we'll figure out how to connect the nodes. If we get into trouble, you, Dadeus, and Mary can guide us."

The adults all started to protest in a rowdy uproar, until John knelt before his son. "Are you sure this is the only solution to this problem?"

"Yes, I am."

"From what we've learned over the past couple of hours, this is a battle for the future of The Balance and the World as we know it. I…we can't help but worry for your safety. You're going to try to do something that has never been done before. Considering the state you're in at the moment, are you sure you have the strength for this?"

Alius interrupted. "I have to talk with my father before I go. What if we left in the morning?"

"I'll agree to that," moaned Adrian.

Ponte interrupted, "I have one more question that should be answered this evening, so I can do a little research before you two start on your journey. Where are the seven nodes?"

"Rome, Jerusalem, The Sphinx, The Forbidden City in Beijing, The Lincoln Memorial in Washington, Stonehenge, and the headwaters of the Amazon River in Peru."

"We'll see what we can find out tonight and pass this along to Gabrielle and Dadeus. They might have different insights."

John wrapped his arms around his son, "I love you." He picked the boy up and carried him out to the trolley.

Adrian awoke to bright sunshine seeping in around the curtains billowing at his window. He dressed in his blue robes from La Isla de los Ninas, which had large pockets to carry his key and the little pocketknife, and strode down to the kitchen, feeling surprisingly strong and ready for the journey.

Everyone else was seated around the table. His mother rose to hug him, "Are you hungry?"

"I'm starved!" smiled Adrian.

His father said, "We want to drive you up to the Professor's house. Save your strength."

"Alright."

The girls both stared at Adrian. There were no giggles to mask their concern. "You've done a lot of incredible things and we're very proud of you...but this one sounds much more dangerous than the rest," said Molly through a mouthful of muffin.

"Is there anything we can do to help?" asked Megan.

Adrian thought for a moment, "You know, there is something you can do. We believe that Sir Winston, our visitor the other day, transferred from that yacht to a small submarine. I've been wondering whether Zepallo's people are moving around the world in little subs. Could you ask Spot and Dusty to ask the sea creatures to look out for them and, perhaps, make their travels a little less comfortable? They might even be able to tell us where their Ice Island is located."

Molly and Megan smiled, "Sure!"

Adrian devoured his breakfast amid a raucous voicing of opinions and ideas about what was about to happen. Finally, he raised his hand, "The one thing I want you all to know is that I love you very much. You are the people that mean the most to me and this way of life is worth the journey that I'm about to take."

Everyone was quiet until Elsie said, "We all love you, too, and we'll worry about you until you're safely back under this roof… preferably in one piece."

Adrian smiled, picked up his dishes, and carried them to the sink, "I think it's time to go."

The twins headed for the cove in the wagon while George, John, Sara, and Adrian piled into the trolley and headed north. Jofre, Alius, Mandor, Nanchez and Alius' aunt, Aileen, were just getting out of their vehicles, when the trolley pulled up to the observatory.

Jofre walked over and offered a large hand to help Adrian out of the back of the trolley. He squatted in front of the boy, his white eyes boring into Adrian's soul. "I've talked with the Professor and Nanchez about what you're about to attempt and why you want Alius to accompany you. I understand the lust for power and the mesmerizing influence of the Black Crystals and I'm ashamed to admit that I dreamed of the potential they promised. A few months ago, I couldn't have appreciated any of this but you two children showed us a better way. I have to support you in any way I can, including allowing my daughter to face a danger that I can't quite comprehend. I trust that you will look after her?"

"I'll do my best but she is a fine *seer* in her own right."

Jofre stood, white eyes staring down at Adrian for a long moment, before guiding him with a heavy hand on his shoulder, as they walked up the steps and through the front door. Adrian felt tiny and meek next to this giant man.

They descended to the white room, before the Golden Crystal, and everyone gathered around Adrian and Alius.

Alius looked nervous. Adrian took both of her hands in his and said, "Look into my eyes. I know where we're going. I can see it in my mind. There's a large plaza made of white stone surrounded by the ruins of ancient buildings. To the north is a stepped pyramid growing out of lush green jungle. It looks almost pink in the sunshine. Do not resist the image but allow your energy to flow into it. I don't want to be separated from you as we move along this path. We are joined together, traveling as one." He squeezed her hands, "Do you hear the vibration?"

Alius looked deeply into his eyes. She opened her mind to his vision and concentrated every ounce of energy through Adrian to their destination. She felt their powers merging. "Yes."

"Hold on tight," smiled Adrian. A moment later, they vanished.

The young *seer* clutched Alius with all his might. He was almost afraid that he might hurt her but he could not let go. He always felt drained when he entered the Crystals but this sensation filled his body with energy.

The lights streamed past and the low rumble of the vibrations carried them along without resistance, in spite of the speed. Adrian sensed the movement and, yet, felt as if he was standing still and everything else was surging past. Suddenly, there was a flash and violent bump but the colored streamers returned. "We just passed through a Crystal."

The corners of Alius' lips curled nervously.

Another flash and then another, and, suddenly, they were standing on a hard surface. The movement stopped but the sensation still raced through their bodies and they steadied each other for a moment.

"Dizzy?"

"Yeah," gasped Alius.

"Me, too, but it'll pass in a minute."

They looked around at the structures surrounding the plaza. Adrian was amazed that they all looked as if they were being built, rather than falling down. Piles of white rock were neatly stacked, here and there, and he noticed mason's tools near one of the smaller structures.

He turned around to gaze at the pyramid rising out of the forest to the north above the entrance to the cave where they stayed with the other children. The sun was just rising in the east, puffy pink clouds drifted through the dark blue sky, and the plaza was deserted.

He thought for a moment, *"They haven't started yet, they're at breakfast!"*

He turned to Alius, "We're here! Come on, I'll show you the way."

Alius resisted, turning around and around to take in the buildings and the forest, "This is beautiful. Was this little city built by the people who escaped from Central America?"

"Yes. The history says there was a terrific battle with the pirates, who destroyed these buildings and forced the survivors to flee underground."

Adrian led Alius up the path and through the jungle to the waterfall. Blackbeard, the monkey, was sitting on a rock at the edge of the pool. "I thought you left with the boat?"

"Well, I did but now I'm back. How are you? And when did you learn to speak English?"

"Oh, it's much more fun now that the humans understand The Balance. Everyone is helping everyone else. All the animals have learned to speak your tongue. We keep wondering when you will learn to speak ours?"

"That'll take a while!"

Blackbeard scurried over and climbed up into Adrian's arms, "It's nice to see you. You should introduce me to your beautiful friend!"

"I'm sorry, Blackbeard, this my fellow *seer* from Morgan's Knot, Alius. Alius, this is Blackbeard."

Alius shook the little monkey's hand and said, "It's nice to meet you!"

Blackbeard reached out to grab a fistful of her straight white hair, "You have beautiful hair. I've never seen snow but your hair is the color I imagine snow should be."

"Leave her alone!" laughed Adrian. "Is everyone up yet?"

"Yes. They're all in the dining dome. I'll show you the way!" said the little monkey, jumping down to scamper along the path and up the rocks to the entrance behind the waterfall.

Adrian grabbed Alius' hand and followed, "You'll love this!"

They chased Blackbeard down into the tunnels and through the airlock to the first dome. Alius stopped and stared around the bubble and then at the ocean beyond the structure. She walked over to a window and peered out at fish swimming just outside the glass, "This is magical!"

"Yes, it really is." Adrian picked up the monkey and the two *seers* turned into a glass tunnel across to the dining dome. Everyone in the room stopped talking and turned to stare when they stepped through the lock.

"Look who I found!" exclaimed Blackbeard.

Raffe, Gabrielle, and Mary all jumped up and ran over to give Adrian a hug.

"How did you get here?" asked Raffe, grinning from ear to ear.

"I'm going to teach you how to move along the vectors. We have a mission."

"And who is this," asked Gabrielle, reaching to grasp Alius' hand.

"I'm sorry, this is my fellow *seer* from Morgan's Knot. Allow me to introduce Alius. This is Raffe, Gabrielle, and Mary."

Alius curtsied and gazed around the room, her eyes wandering across the panorama of ocean. The *orbs* on the outside of the structure enhanced the brilliant colors of the corals along the reef, the entire panorama shimmering with life against an infinitely dark background. Sharks moved past the windows, schools of rainbow chubb swarmed together into a shimmering cloud, and barracuda snapped at the strays. Alius' face glowed with the most wondrous look of enchantment.

Adrian smiled. "Isn't this fantastic?"

"Now I understand what you were trying to explain. The elders on Morgan's Knot need to understand the magic of this place!"

Suddenly, Dadeus rushed into the dome and stopped short, when he spied Adrian. "Oh, my! Ponte just called to tell me that you were coming…but you're already here!"

Adrian walked over to hug the bald man. "I've learned some new tricks!"

"I can see that!"

Mary said, "Come join us for breakfast, there's plenty!"

Alius smiled, "Thank you but we've just had a meal a little while ago." She looked at Adrian, "I'm not really sure how long ago. It almost seemed that time stood still as we moved along the vectors."

Adrian grinned, "That's another puzzle."

They followed Gabrielle and sat down at the table. Dadeus pulled up a chair. "If I understand Nanchez and the Professor correctly, we have a tyrant, named Zepallo, who is trying to connect all of the dark vectors together. We've been following the hurricane and it seems to be aiming for Jamaica. Like Ponte and Nanchez, our instruments indicate that it is man-made."

Adrian nodded.

"You're seeking seven identical Ruby Crystals and planning to find each of the nodes to insert one Crystal in each?"

"That is correct."

"Ponte told me about the talents of your new friend, Simian?"

"Yes, he found us or we found him in Jamaica. In many ways, he's a novice *seer* but he knows things we never even considered. He can move along the vectors and taught us how to do it."

"I see. And that's how you arrived here this morning?"

"Yes."

"No matter how much we learn, there is more," Dadeus shook his head. "I can provide the gems. Ponte said that they have to be about the same size as the Balancing Crystal and I happen to have just what you need."

"Great," replied Adrian. "The sooner we begin this mission, the sooner we'll all be safe."

He turned to Raffe, "You said you wanted to learn everything that there was to know about the Powers and the Crystals. The more *seers* who help with this mission, the easier it'll be."

"I'm ready to learn," smiled Raffe.

"We need someplace quiet, where we can talk," said Adrian.

"The pyramid," laughed Raffe, "Let's go!"

Mary stood and said, "I'm going too. Alius needs a robe and you three need the supervision of an adult *seer*!

The four moved through the tunnels to the pyramid and Mary produced a robe for Alius along the way. Adrian was amazed at the change. *Orbs* had been installed in the ceiling to illuminate the story etched on the walls. Desks were lined up in neat rows in four distinct areas of the space with bookcases as dividers between the open classrooms. The cases were stuffed with books.

"Where did you get all the books?"

"Quite a few of them were used in the old classrooms, where we taught the new arrivals, but we've added to the collection, since we started trading with the mainland. We'll never have enough books!" smiled Mary.

They dragged four chairs to the center of the room beneath the open slots in the peak. "Okay. There's a man named Zepallo who is merging the dark vectors together into a network of extreme energies. The hurricane, that's heading for Jamaica, is a demonstration of his power. If he's allowed to complete the web, he'll have absolute control over all the power in the world. The only way to stop his progress is to connect all of the Positive Crystals together through a series of seven nodes."

Raffe and Mary nodded before Adrian continued, "We've learned to travel along the vectors and we'll teach you how to do it. Each of us will take a couple of Ruby Crystals and deposit them in the node Crystals," indicating Raffe and Alius, "Mary, you and Dadeus can stay in touch with Ponte and Nanchez to monitor the systems and direct our paths."

Mary interrupted, "You say that you can transport yourselves along the vectors. How does that work?"

Adrian and Alius grinned, "It's easy for a *seer*. Have you noticed the low rumble when you're close to the Crystal or one of the stronger vectors?"

Raffe smiled, "Yeah, I know that sound, it's always in the background. The only way I can describe it is that it's like rumbling thunder at a great distance. You can't really hear it but you feel it in your gut."

"That's it. I always thought that it was something inside my head when I first started studying the Books," commented Alius. "Something that you try not to pay attention to, even though you're aware of it in the backgroun...except the dark vectors make a different...I don't know how to describe it...edgy...grating...irritating sound. The tone of the positive vectors is smoother."

"We all hear that sound," said Mary. "What's the next step?"

"How about a small demonstration?"

"Okay!" grinned Raffe.

Adrian and Alius stood. "We'll take you to the plaza, to show you how it feels. You'll have a little bit of dizziness when you land but it passes quickly. Concentrate on the center of the plaza."

Raffe and Mary stood and Adrian and Alius placed their hands on their shoulders, closed their eyes, and concentrated on the sound and their destination. A moment later, they were all standing in the middle of the plaza. Mary and Raffe gazed around and giggled. "That's fantastic!" laughed Mary. "I saw colored lights streaming past us."

"I'm not really sure what those are but don't be concerned."

"They're beautiful," said Raffe.

The four *seers* looked up at the brilliant sky. The lush jungle almost seemed to be leaning into the plaza. A chorus of bird songs echoed around the stone square and the air was filled with the fragrant scent of flowers.

Alius inhaled the delicate perfume and smiled. "Okay, now let's try to go back to the classroom in the pyramid. Close your eyes and listen for the sound. Do you hear it?"

Raffe and Mary both nodded. "Now concentrate on the classroom and where you want to land. Be very precise. You don't want to end up inside a wall or under the floor!"

"I can see the four chairs," said Raffe.

"The sound will become more intense, as you concentrate. When you see yourself in our destination, let go," whispered Adrian.

Suddenly, they were standing together in the pyramid, their arrival announced by a loud clatter as Raffe plowed through the chairs.

"You might be concentrating a little too hard on the chairs," laughed Alius.

Mary had a huge smile, "The wonders of the powers never end. There is always more to learn!"

"It seems that the system runs through the nodes. The positive Crystals are loosely connected together but, at this point, when we traveled here, we passed through other Crystals on our way and felt several large bumps. I'm hoping that, when all of the nodes are connected together, we'll be able to move directly from one place to another instead of bouncing from one overlapping set of vectors to the next."

Gabrielle and Dadeus entered the pyramid and, from the look on the faces of the four *seers*, wondered whether they were dealing with three children or four.

"Did we miss something?" asked Dadeus.

Mary tried to contain her smile, "We'll have to take you along the vectors. It is so much fun!"

Gabrielle shook his head. His long beard flowed back and forth. "Sit down, all of you. There's much to discuss."

The elders pulled up two more chairs to fill in the circle. "I've located the Ruby Crystals that you will need," said Dadeus. "We've talked with Ponte and there are some things that you should know about each of the destinations that you'll be visiting."

"The list that you provided is rather interesting. For the most part, these are places that represent man's interaction and conflicts within the spiritual world. The lone exception is the headwaters of the Amazon. Perhaps that one influenced the societies of the Incas and the Mayans but was never really discovered or used directly because it appears relatively remote and inaccessible. The others are significant and unique in several ways and I think that it would benefit each of you to understand them before you head off across the vectors," said Gabrielle with the tone of a teacher trying to convince a class of the importance of the subject that they were about to study.

Dadeus added, "Adrian, you and Alius have studied history in school and you're probably aware of the significance of most of these places. Raffe is just beginning to learn about these things, so bear with us."

The three young *seers* nodded.

Dadeus continued, "We've done some research and, when combined with the information that Ponte and Nanchez have supplied, we've reached some conclusions."

"First, by tracing the vectors, we can pinpoint the location of each of the nodes and we'll be able to help you reach your destinations...but...we have also learned that each of the nodes is paired with a Black Crystal. Each of these places is viewed as a positive center of the spiritual world but with each positive there have also been negatives."

"Let's use Rome as an example, once capitol of an ancient empire that stretched from the Atlantic to Persia, from Africa to Scotland. Certainly, they fought, plundered, and enslaved millions as the realm expanded but they also developed things like urban planning and monumental construction methods that are still the model for contemporary cities," said Gabrielle. "St. Peter's is the heart of The Church and, if you stretch a little bit, the nucleus of the Christian world.

The Pope is viewed, in some western religions, as being the closest living being to God and millions of people in every part of the world see the Vatican as the touchstone of heaven."

"When the Roman Empire moved from paganism to Christianity, the writings of the Apostles were edited by the Emperor and his people to reinforce their political control over the population. In the process, they stripped away some of the writings that explained the humanity of Jesus Christ and included only those that portrayed him purely as a God. In the process, they changed the equilibrium between man and woman and man and nature. Many beautiful and meaningful chapters of the story were left out."

"The dark side of that tale is that, over the past two thousand years, The Church has not always been on the right side of certain moral and political issues. I'll suggest that the Inquisition led to the torture and deaths of thousands of people, who were not necessarily guilty of anything. There are many other examples, throughout history, but my point here is that the impact of each of the paired Crystals has had an influence on the course of mankind's saga. You'll have to be very careful to find the Positive Crystals without disturbing the Black Crystals."

Raffe asked, "What was the Inquisition?"

Mary replied, "It was a court system set up by the Church to find and punish non-believers. It was a case of 'Believe as we instruct you to believe or you will pay with your life. There will be no dissent.' In ancient times, the clergy and the aristocracy were the only members of their societies who could read, so, the Bible, the word of God, was interpreted by the clergy for the commoners. That arrangement gave great power to The Church and reinforced the aristocracy. Religion could calm their souls while the gentry collected their taxes and controlled everything else."

"Our belief in The Balance is a good example. Those who believed in the powers of the Crystals and The Balance between man and nature were branded as witches or heretics and many were tortured and burned at the stake. From what I learned from John and Sara,

Captain Morgan collected a number of families and took them to an island that was conveniently excluded from the nautical charts of the time. They were free to live by their own beliefs and the result was Morgan's Knot."

Raffe thought for a moment, "So, on the one hand, the Church represents the foundation of western religion but, on the other, the source of spiritual truth is not always honest?"

"In a way," replied Gabrielle. "An understanding of the history of The Church leads us to believe that there is both a positive and a negative influence. People who believe in the teachings of The Church believe in the best of Christian traditions and that is admirable. My example is not intended to take anything from people who have faith in their religions. Faith and belief allow us to expand beyond what we can see and touch to accept what our hearts know to be true. Unfortunately, there is another, very human side, that led some leaders to choose a dark path instead of a righteous one. There is a positive and a negative because there are two Crystals... one dark and the other light."

Mary continued, "These are places where man has reached a new level of understanding of the world around them and about the spiritual universe. In almost every case, Man made great leaps forward on the basis of things that were learned or created near these sites. Unfortunately, there were also evil things that happened along the way. Every human faces choices throughout their lives, some choose to turn towards the light and others turn the other way. Each of us is influenced by the beliefs of the society that we inhabit but it is up to each individual to choose the path that they will ultimately follow."

Alius asked, "How about the Lincoln Memorial in Washington?"

Mary smiled, "Lincoln represents the very best of intentions and goals but he also had to deal with the fact that his conviction and determination led to a war between the North and the South...brother against brother. There was a very high price to pay for trying to lead his country to a new understanding of the human condition and, once again, it was a conflict of two very distinct sets of beliefs."

"What about the head-waters of the Amazon?" asked Adrian.

Gabrielle pondered his response before he spoke. "I don't know the answer to your question. That is the one that stands out as being different from the others. It could be that the Incas and the Mayans built their empires around Crystals that were tied together through the powers emanating from that node but I would guess it was never discovered, let alone developed."

"Let's touch on the others," said Dadeus. "Jerusalem is the spiritual center for Christians, Jews, and Muslims, yet it is also the point at which the beliefs of all these different religions clash. Each has a claim to overlapping parts of the city. Over the centuries, many wars have been fought for dominance and liberation of the 'holy land' and I doubt that it would surprise anyone if there were more conflicts for that tiny piece of sacred history."

"The Sphinx doesn't surprise me. The Egyptian empire succumbed to new beliefs taking the place of their ancient understanding of The Balance," said Mary. "Beijing is the capitol of a nation with several billion citizens and their continuous history goes back farther than in any other culture in the world. It was one of the first places where a modern society developed and continued to thrive. The Forbidden City was viewed as the center of the universe and the most powerful spot in the empire, so it's little wonder that they chose to build it on top of the Crystals."

The three children were quiet for a few minutes, while they digested the ideas that the elders had presented. "Perhaps, each of us should choose one node, to start with, and then we can proceed to the rest," suggested Adrian.

"I agree," said Gabrielle. "To save arguments, I will choose the first stop for each of you. Alius, you will take the Lincoln Memorial. Raffe, you will go to the Sphinx, and, Adrian, you will go to Rome. When you have completed your missions, you will return here and then we can go on to the next three. Is that alright with each of you?"

The three *seers* nodded their consent.

Dadeus had been quiet for a while, "I have one more tool that will help you to find the exact location of the Crystals." He pulled three pairs of glasses from his pocket and held them up.

"These look like ordinary glasses. Please put them on. You'll see that they allow you to see the vectors and, when you reach your destinations, you'll find that all of the vectors come together at a point. That is where you will find the node."

The *seers* put the glasses on.

"Wow," said Alius. "They look like long slender golden clouds. They vibrate and glow!"

Raffe gasped, "I can see vectors branching out from our Crystal like the spokes of a wheel, only they're curved and snake around!"

Adrian just grinned. He could feel the vectors and now he could see them, "This is fantastic. We should be able to find them in a snap!"

Dadeus smiled, "Now touch the right arm of the frame of the glasses."

The children touched the right side of their glasses, "What are we supposed to…? I can hear myself!"

"I can hear you too," said Alius. "Will we be able to communicate with each other?"

"Yes, and with us," said Dadeus. "Now touch the left side. The special lenses of these glasses also transmit an image of what you are looking at. You should be able to see what the others are seeing. I haven't perfected this yet, so the pictures are fairly small and a bit faint."

The children turned to look at different parts of the room, "I can see what I am seeing in both eyes and I can see what Adrian is seeing in my left eye and what Raffe is seeing in my right. This is great!"

Dadeus smiled, "I'm hoping that it will allow each of you to help the others and that it will let us contribute from the lab. You can turn off the communications by touching both arms of the glasses."

"I'm feeling a bit more confident," said Raffe. "Let's go!"

Alius reached into the pocket of her robes and withdrew three black crystals on golden chains. "Nanchez suggested that we wear these as protection against the dark powers. He might have a point." She handed one to Adrian and the other to Raffe, who slipped them around their necks.

Chapter 19

Zepallo turned slowly, gazing at giant screens encircling the huge room. One by one, the black vectors were being connected into a super web of dark energy. *"Step by step, little by little, our progress is relentless,"* he thought, his mouth straining into a sinister grimace.

His black cape flared as he whirled around to the three displays at the front of the room. The one on the left presented the international news churning one disaster after another. His emissaries were guiding the leaders of the world towards a precipice from which they would tumble, on his command, like lemmings dropping off a cliff into the cold dark sea. When everything started to unravel, he would step forward as the savior, leading the Dark Forces to triumph in spite of the timidity of the tottering Masters of the Council.

The center panel mapped a global view of the growing web of connections and the third followed the track of the hurricane, spiraling west-north-west, aiming to rake along the length of the island of Jamaica. After crossing Cuba into the Florida Straits, it would regain strength as it moved into open waters before veering north to spin up the west coast of the peninsula.

The storm was large enough to fill the entire Gulf of Mexico and its eye was a tight void whipping swirling tentacles around the core. The first arms would soon sweep across the Dominican Republic and Haiti, to ravage the eastern tip of Jamaica. Surging surf, lashing winds, and torrential rains would buffet the islands and tornadoes would appear, here and there, clearing swaths of devastation through the lush tropical paradise.

"No man can stop this power," thought Zepallo. "Sir Winston! It is time to call our emissaries together for one final meeting. Send out the message and deploy the subs to pick them up. As our connections are

completed and events begin to accelerate around the world, there will not be another opportunity to meet. It is time!"

Sir Winston bowed and moved to a workstation to send out the codes that would draw the flock to their shepherd.

Chapter 20

Dadeus supplied a ruby crystal and a small *orb* to each of the *seers*, which they placed in the pockets of their robes, and Mary produced a key for Raffe.

Adrian turned to Alius and Raffe, "You've watched me enter the Crystals but I don't think I've told you the procedure."

"Nope, I was astonished that you survived," replied Raffe.

He paused to organize the sequence in his mind, a terrifying progression that was rapidly becoming a grueling routine. "Insert your key. A voice will ask whether you are a *seer*. Identify yourself and answer the question, then remove your key. When the hole opens, step through it. You'll be standing on a tiny flat pad, in the middle of a crystal tornado. The gem seems to spin faster on the inside and the figures from the Books wander all over the inner surface. A globe will appear that shows the world, as it was when the oceans receded to reveal the land. The continents will slowly pull apart and move into the positions that they occupy now and the locations of the Crystals will glimmer red and black. A very large voice will ask how it can help. Simply respond that you have been sent to install a ruby crystal to connect all the nodes and Crystals in the world. If it asks you why, tell the truth…that there is an evil force that is trying to connect all the Black Crystals. It will instruct you on what to do next."

"What about your energy level?" asked Alius. "You always pass out when you come out of the Crystal."

"I honestly don't know what to tell you. This encounter shouldn't take too long and perhaps my reaction has had something to do with how long I spent inside the Crystals. I've also noticed that traveling on the vectors seems to add energy, so maybe they'll even out," replied Adrian.

"You'll want to retrace your steps as soon as you've finished installing the ruby crystals. First, because we don't want any of you getting into trouble outside the Crystals, and second, we're running against a deadline. The hurricane is moving west-north-west. Jamaica is dead in its path and time is running out," said Gabrielle.

"Then we should begin," said Raffe.

"Alright. We'll instruct each of you on where to go once you arrive and, for the moment, I think that we'll direct all communications through Dadeus. Adrian, you're aiming for the floor of the St. Peter's Basilica in the Vatican in Rome. Raffe, find the space between the paws of the Sphinx. Alius you want to land on the steps in front of the Memorial." He turned to the boys, "If you two leave now, you'll arrive in the middle of the night. We'll hold up on sending Alius, to allow the Memorial to be secured for the evening."

Adrian and Raffe stepped forward. "Do you have the ruby crystal, your key, the *orb*, and the glasses?" asked Dadeus.

The boys reached into their pockets and displayed the four objects for the elders. Raffe leaned to hug Adrian. "Good luck!"

"Are you sure you're comfortable with what you have to do?"

"I'm sure," smiled Raffe. "I feel as if I always knew that I could do this. I just didn't know how."

The boys closed their eyes to concentrate on the low rumble of the vibrations and their destinations. A moment later, they vanished.

Adrian opened his eyes in a rush of streaming colors whizzing past at an astonishing speed. He listened to the tone and found it almost musical, rising and descending as he moved along. He imagined a bow, running across the strings of a cello, creating a smooth, round tenor. A flash and a bump interrupted the sensation and then the sound returned. *"Percussion instruments!"*

Another bump, and then another, before his feet were planted on a smooth marble aisle stretching through the grand chapel, dark, save spotlights on the huge Alter and sculptures in nooks around the edges of the enormous room. He gaped at the huge curling columns reaching for the ceiling like enormous vines at the corners of the Alter, completely awed by the sheer size of the cathedral. Angels and saints peered down from the ceiling, each panel or statue a narrative of the relationship between man and his God. The figures seemed to grow from normal human proportions to colossal, as the chapters unfolded around him. Images adorned every surface and gleaming white marble sculptures glowed in alcoves, which made him pause, wondering about the struggle between the darkness and the light in this, the very heart of one of the world's great religions.

The young *seer* padded slowly along the floor, feeling small and insignificant in an allee of giant columns soaring to support arches marching across the ceiling. Everything was out of scale and every surface was beautiful, demanding reverence.

"No wonder people from every corner of the world come here to worship, just being in this place is awesome," thought Adrian. *"This is magnificently overwhelming!"* He stopped and listened but there was no sound to hear, save a faint whisper of air moving, and, certainly, no other people in the chapel. Adrian focused on the Alter and the enormous dome rising to a peak hundreds of feet above the floor. He pulled the glasses from his pocket and, suddenly, the room glimmered with curved, flowing vectors surging from somewhere below the Alter. He touched the right arm of the glasses and then the left, "Can you see what I'm seeing?"

Gabrielle's voice crackled, "Well done! Now, listen carefully. When this church was constructed, they built the Alter directly under the precipice of the dome. Officially, they claim they didn't know at the time but, somehow, discovered that St. Peter was buried, centuries before, directly under the Alter. I would guess that there is a Positive Crystal on one side of his grave and a Black Crystal on the other. Directly behind the Alter, you'll find several columns. Behind them is a single unremarkable door. Enter and it appears that you will find a staircase."

Adrian walked around the magnificent Alter, feeling that he should bow, if only to show his respect for those who built this wonder and those who came here to worship. Tucked in the shadows of the giant columns, Adrian found the single, non-descript door and was amazed to find that it was not locked.

A tiny squeak made him freeze for a moment before ducking down a spiral stairway, lit only by a single shaft of light spilling down through the center. He leaned over the railing to find an endless coil of stairs unwinding into a dark pit. Vectors swirled around the well and he wondered whether the dark streaks might be intersections where the positive and negative powers crossed paths.

He landed at one end of a long chamber and trudged past countless layers of dark caves, carved into each wall, with small plaques identifying the ancient burial crypts of Popes and Saints. At the far end of the catacombs, the boy found another set of stairs descending to a deeper level below the burial chamber. He scrambled down the staircase to find a narrow hallway. The end of the tunnel was bounded by three heavy wooden doors. He inspected each panel, they were all exactly the same.

Mary's voice appeared, "It seems that we have to make a choice. If Gabrielle's theory is correct, the center door will be the crypt of St. Peter."

"The positive vectors all seem to be coming from the door on the left," said Adrian.

"Then try the door on your left." Alius' voice was quiet, confident, and slightly sarcastic.

There was an odd but familiar keyhole but no door handle, so he withdrew his key and inserted it in the slot. As it linked, he felt a tiny tingling in his fingers and pushed on the door. It opened with a creak, revealing a tiny man in long tattered robes, who rose from a small stool at the center of a rough stone floor in a barren room to face him.

"Who are you?"

"I am Adrian. I'm a *seer* who has been sent to save the Crystal."

"There is nothing wrong with the Crystal," said the tiny man.

"Who are you?" asked Adrian.

"I am the Keeper of the Powers. I live here."

"Do you have a name?"

"They call me Equus."

"How long have you been down here?" asked Adrian.

"I was a young man when I first descended into this shrine," said Equus, hooking a thumb over his shoulder. "My neighbor gets few visitors and I fewer still. It is not often that I climb those stairs to feel sunlight on my face."

Adrian considered the little priest, "There's an evil man who's trying to connect all of the Black Crystals. If he succeeds, he'll control all of the power in the world."

The tiny man gazed at Adrian with disbelief, "How do I know you're not here on his behalf?"

"You don't but I have a ruby crystal that I would like to install in the Golden Crystal and I have a key that will allow me to enter. If this is like the other Crystals that I have visited, there will be a small slot in the base beneath the Crystal."

The little man eyed Adrian, "Are you a Christian?"

The boy stared bashfully at the floor for a moment, "I went to church with my parents when I was younger but I honestly don't know what I believe about God and The Church. That's something that I'm still trying to figure out. I know that I believe in The Balance between man and nature and that I'd give my life to preserve the best of the world around us."

"That is an honest answer," said the little man, staring into the young *seer's* eyes. Adrian noticed that his robes were threadbare and a small worn cross, hanging from a rosary around his neck, shimmered in the glow of the Golden Crystal bursting from a cavern at the far end of a short hallway. He was barefoot.

"If I were on a mission to connect the Black Crystals, I would have entered the door on the right. I'm assuming there's a Black Crystal behind that door."

"You are correct. What is behind the door in the middle?"

"I'm told it's the grave of St. Peter."

Equus bowed his head, crossed himself, and then looked up at Adrian. "You are the first person, other than the kitchen help who deliver my meals, who has entered this chamber since I arrived and I have every reason to keep you from the Crystal. I've dedicated my life to defending this secret…but I have no idea what the real world is like in these times and I sense that you are telling the truth. I understand the secrets of the stones but I can't say the same about mankind."

"There are seven of these Crystals that control the connections to all of the positive Crystals in the world. We believe that the combined powers of the positive Crystals will be stronger than the powers of the Black Crystals and that our Keepers will be able to stop Zepallo from taking over the world."

"Did you say Zepallo?" asked the little man, concern wrinkling his brow.

"We believe that the man behind all of this is named Zepallo."

"That's a name I've not heard since I was a young man."

"Who is he?"

"The man that I knew claimed he was born in Jerusalem, although his English was more fluent than his Yiddish, became a priest, and rose through the hierarchy of the Church. He ended up in the Holy City, as a special envoy for the Pope, and it was whispered that he would someday rise to take the Papal throne. He oversaw the protection of the Crystals and, for someone his age, wielded immense power. No one knows what happened to him. He didn't leave the Vatican, he just disappeared."

Gabrielle's voice erupted in Adrian's ear, "That's interesting!"

The little man mused, "Even in the holiest of temples, the hallways are paced by the devout, the ambitious and, certainly, the corrupt. I find it hard to believe that directing the reach of the entire ministry and worldwide adoration was not enough to satisfy his thirst for power."

"It seems that he wants it all, not just a big chunk, so you have every reason to help me," said Adrian.

The little man pondered the situation for a moment, "I am at your service."

Adrian pulled off his glasses and walked through a small alcove to the immense stone turning slowly a foot above the floor. It was the same golden color as the Crystal on Morgan's Knot, although much larger. He knelt down and brushed the gold dust away from the plinth beneath the stone to reveal the slot.

Equus crawled under the stone to inspect the small opening, "I always wondered what that was but I never considered that it might be a keyhole!"

Adrian withdrew the key from his pocket and held it out for the little man to inspect.

"That is an ancient symbol."

"We believe that it represents The Balance between man and nature," said Adrian quietly.

The little man returned the key to Adrian's hand. The young *seer* leaned to insert it in the slot. A large, booming voice asked, "Who seeks entry?"

"I am Adrian. I am a *seer!*" He withdrew his key and returned it to his pocket.

The little man backed away, as Crystal rotated faster and faster, his eyes wide and his mouth hanging open in astonishment. A large dark area appeared on the side of the stone and Adrian stepped inside the giant gem. The inner surface swirled higher than any other Crystal Adrian had entered and a stout wind whirled around with a menacing whistle.

The figures moved away from the center of his view and the globe appeared. The continents moved apart and the voice asked, "How may We help you?"

"I am here on a mission to connect all of the nodes together," said Adrian.

"Why would you want to tie all of the nodes together?"

"There is an evil man who is linking all of the dark vectors and, soon, he'll have more power than anyone on earth. We have to stop him."

"We have felt this disruption," said the voice.

"I brought a ruby crystal to install. I was told that when these crystals have been inserted in all seven nodes, we'll be able to connect the positive powers together to overcome this evil."

"That is correct."

The globe disappeared and was replaced by a series of concentric circles receding to a point at infinity. Each loop pulsed a different color, static electric rings skittering into oblivion. Adrian pulled the ruby crystal from his robes and reached to insert the gem in the center of the image.

The voice asked, "Do you believe in The Balance?"

"Yes, I do."

"Then let go."

Adrian released the ruby crystal and the colored circles closed around it. A blinding flash erupted from the center of the cone and the gem disappeared.

"Your mission is complete. There are six nodes left and we sense that the dark powers are increasing. You must hurry!"

The murky blotch appeared to his right and he stepped through it, feeling faint and queasy, and staggered as he stepped on the floor of the chamber. Equus offered a hand to steady the young *seer*, "Are you alright? That was the most amazing thing I've ever seen. I might almost call it a miracle!"

Adrian took a deep breath and tried to regain his balance, "I'll be alright in a minute. It takes an incredible amount of energy but it is no miracle. I think the people upstairs are far more qualified in miracles than I'll ever be!"

"You're probably right about that," sighed Equus.

"I'd better go, there are six more nodes that have to be connected and we're running out of time."

"I admire you for what you are trying to accomplish and thank you for coming. It has been so long since I last talked with another human being," the little man smiled, "who wore robes of a different cloth."

"You could always walk up those stairs," said Adrian.

"No, I can never leave the Crystal," sighed the little man, sadly. "That is my duty just as your journey calls to you. I will pray for you but it is time to go."

Adrian shook his hand and turned to leave.

"Godspeed," said Equus.

"Thank you," replied Adrian. "I'll accept that as a blessing."

He opened the door and turned down the hallway, up the steps, through the dank and eerie burial chambers, up the endless spiral staircase, and into the chapel. He closed the door gently and treaded silently around the Alter, turning for one last look and a bow in respect for the little man's dedication to his beliefs. *This is truly amazing!"*

A shout echoed around the enormous chapel and banks of lights flashed on, one after another, from the far end of the aisle. He closed his eyes, concentrating on the tone and then the pyramid on the Island of the Children. A moment later, he was gone.

Raffe zoomed along the vectors, fascinated with the streaming colors. The first bump startled him but he relaxed as the tone and flush returned. Another flash before he crashed face first into a mound of sand. He flailed around in panic, spitting a mouthful of grit, until he glanced up into the enormous face of the Sphinx. The nose and part of the cheek were broken off long ago but it was an imposing face of calm regal power. He realized that the huge sculpture embodied a man's head on a lion's torso. *"He sure must have been an important person,"* thought Raffe.

The moon was almost full and the sky was blazing with stars as he crept out from between colossal paws to peer along each flank of the beast to three enormous pyramids without spying anyone nearby. He pulled the glasses from the pocket of his robes and put them on. Iridescent vectors swirled around the head of the Sphinx, erupting from a point where the lion's heart might have been. He touched both arms of the glasses and Gabrielle's voice crackled in his ear.

"Well done! No one is quite certain when the Sphinx was built or who it actually represents. Some archeologists have proposed that it is the face of young Tut's grandfather but the best estimate is that it was constructed long before the pyramids and they are four and a half thousand years old."

"I almost feel that I can see back through time. I want to learn a lot more about the Egyptians!"

"There will be time for that. Now, walk straight between the paws. You should find a stone plaque directly beneath the chin of the Sphinx."

Raffe walked between the paws until he was standing before a tall stone tablet, installed before the chest of the beast. He ran his hands over engraved writings on the stones but he didn't feel anything that might be a keyhole.

"Crawl around the stone and look directly beneath the Sphinx's chin," said Dadeus quietly.

Raffe got down on hands and knees and started brushing sand away from the base of the monument. He was leaning into the small crater before his fingers brushed against a hollow in the stone. "I think I've found it!"

He pulled the key from his pocket and inserted it into the hole. He turned it to the left but it wouldn't budge, so he reversed it and felt movement. The stones above his head started grinding, pelting the novice *seer* with petrified mortar and small shards of rock. He pulled the key from the slot and scrambled back. Three large stones swung away from the Sphinx like a gaping wound and he stepped inside

He pulled the *orb* from his pocket and swept the light across the darkness. There was a narrow tunnel burrowing straight back into the body of the Sphinx. The surfaces of the stones glistened with a clear sticky slime.

At the end of the passageway, he found a narrow flight of steps leading down into a dank nightmare. *"I don't like tight places,"* thought Raffe, sucking air through his teeth to stifle quaking shivers and a queasy stomach. His shoes stuck to the stairs, slippery with the slime covering the walls. *"What is this stuff?"*

With each descending step, he noticed small slugs crawling up the walls and slithering across the ceiling. The farther he went, the larger the slugs. At the last step, he stopped. The floor was writhing. He shined his *orb* around the room and gasped, every surface was undulating with giant pale gray slugs.

He struggled to control his repulsion and a churning gut and peered around to find the glow of the Golden Crystal radiating from a large recess in the stone wall at the far end of the room to his left. He swept the *orb* to the other side of the cavern where a Black Crystal scattered black glitterings in a grotto to his right.

He put his glasses back on and the cave erupted in tangles of magenta and gold vectors writhing like bullwhips flicking charges back and forth, "Are you seeing what I'm seeing?"

"I've never seen a pair of Crystals this close together or the energies interacting. I didn't know it could happen!" exclaimed Dadeus.

"What about these slugs. They're gross but alive, so I can't just walk over them!"

"Well, you could!" Even the static in their connection could not muffle the briefest hint of a grin in the lilt of Gabrielle's voice.

Raffe looked around the room and whispered, very softly, "Do you speak English?"

A voice came back that sounded like a thousand tiny sopranos singing in unison, "We speak every tongue."

Raffe stood absolutely still, "I am Raffe. I am a *seer*. There is an evil man who is trying to tie the powers of all of the Black Crystals together. I'm here to place a ruby crystal in the Golden Crystal to bind all of the positive powers together and counter the dark energies."

"No one has entered this chamber in thousands of years. We are the only inhabitants. Why should we believe you?"

"If I was not a *seer*, how could I have gained entry?"

There was silence for a few moments then the thousand voices sang, "If you are truly a *seer*, then you have no need to walk to the Golden Crystal. You should be able to make that journey without touching the floor or injuring any of us."

Raffe pondered his options. *"If I can travel over thousands of miles, I guess I ought to be able to follow the vectors to the Crystal."* The energies were swirling into the Golden Crystal from every direction and the dark vectors were thrashing wildly, sizzling with blue-black sparks where they crossed. *"Those must be the junctures where the vectors overlap, I better find the right one!"*

He closed his eyes and listened for the tone but there were two overlapping and conflicting sounds. The one that he found comforting during his brief journey along the paths and another that was higher in pitch and grating, like a saw hacking through sheet metal. He concentrated on the low rumble and visualized the area in front of the Golden Crystal. A loud whoosh propelled him across the cave to the giant stone.

"You are a *seer!*" cried the thousand voices.

There were no slugs on the surface beneath the gem. Raffe took a deep breath and crawled over to brush away a gooey glob of gold dust. His hands were shaking but he found the slot and inserted his key. A large voice boomed, "Who seeks entry?"

"I am Raffe and I am a *seer!*"

The Crystal increased speed and a dark area appeared before him. He hesitated for a moment and then leapt inside. The figures from the Book of Natural Balance and the walls of the pyramid marched in formation around the spinning Crystal. A globe appeared and the continents slowly spread apart. Small, gleaming dots appeared here and there across the sphere.

The voice bellowed, "How may We help you?"

"I'm here to install a ruby Crystal. There is a man who is trying to connect all of the Black Crystals. We're hoping that the combined power of the positive Crystals will be strong enough to balance the dark powers."

"We are aware of your mission and the convergence in the dark vectors." Concentric circles of light appeared in front of Raffe and he pulled the ruby crystal from the pocket of his robes. He held it up, wondering what to do, and then timidly thrust it into the center of the smallest circle, fearing that his hand might be sucked into the void.

The voice asked, "Do you believe in The Balance?"

"Yes, I do."

"Release the gem!"

Raffe relaxed his grip and, with a flash, the ruby crystal disappeared.

"Your mission is accomplished. There are five more nodes. It is time for you to leave."

"Thank you," said Raffe. The dark area appeared to his right and he fell through it, feeling faint and exhausted. The room started spinning but he grabbed his knees for balance and noticed a surge of slugs converging beneath the giant Crystal.

The thousand voices chimed, "This cavern contains both the dark and the light. We are subject to both influences and it has been a very long time since we had fresh meat in these chambers."

The giant slugs slithered slowly to surround and cover his feet with slime. His whole body quaked with fear but he closed his eyes, thinking, *"I will not be a first meal for this colony of slugs!"* The boy listened for the tone and visualized the sandy area outside, beneath the chin of the Sphinx, sensing the magnetic pull of the high-pitched whine of the dark vectors. *"Concentrate! There is only one way out of this dungeon!"*

A moment later, he was rolling across the sand between the giant stone paws, as the gaping chasm creaked closed behind him. Every muscle in his body convulsed as he rubbed his shoes around in the sand beneath the chin of the Sphinx and wretched. *"That's just disgusting!"*

Chapter 21

Alius paced around Dadeus' cramped control room, anxious to begin her journey. She watched and listened as the boys worked through their assignments but she could not resist checking the clock, counting down the minutes until she could begin her mission.

Mary wrapped an arm around her shoulder, "Abraham Lincoln was, perhaps, the greatest President of the United States because he faced the forces of good and evil and chose a path that was not easy or popular. In the end, the conflict tore the nation apart but his decisions were based on the spirit and intent of the Founding Fathers and his belief in doing what was best for his country and for his people. It became black and white, without any gray, and his tragic death was a consequence of those beliefs."

Alius responded, "I had to overcome my belief in the...other side to see the beauty and wonder of The Balance, so, in a small way, I think I understand how he felt."

Mary smiled, "You are ready to begin your journey."

Alius took a deep breath, closed her eyes, and concentrated on the tone and her destination. With a whoosh, the little *seer* moved into the realm of the vectors. She opened her eyes and felt the colors rushing past resembled raindrops falling from the heavens as you look straight up into the sky during a storm...except these were vibrant and electric.

She thought about her destination and the man represented by the monument. She felt sorry for the president, for the burden of leading his nation to the point where it broke into factions and thousands died in the resulting war. The photographs in the history books showed a very tall, vibrant man when he entered office, transformed into a grizzled, exhausted leader as the war progressed.

In a way, there was strength in his example. *"If he could see beyond the darkness of civil war to the goal of freedom for all people, then I can do this,"* she thought. Several flashes accompanied large bumps and, without warning, she found herself standing unsteadily at the bottom of a vast stone staircase. At the top, surrounded by huge columns, a gigantic sculpture of the former President, sitting in a large chair, stared out across the reflecting pool. Alius thought that he might be looking into tomorrow while pondering the past and wondered whether other presidents had come here seeking guidance or sanction through all he endured.

She marched up the staircase, dwarfed and awed by the statue. As she reached the top step, she turned to look out across the reflecting pools to the Washington Monument and the Capitol Building in the distance. The view was magnificent. She pulled the glasses from her pocket, put them on, and gasped, as a brilliant swarm of vectors swirled around the monument and descended into the top of the figure's head.

Alius touched the arms of her glasses and heard Gabrielle's voice, "It is splendid, isn't it?"

"It's almost overwhelming. If I didn't have to accomplish our mission, I could stand here and stare into his eyes for a very long time!"

"Alright, let's get on with this, there don't seem to be too many people hanging about. To anyone watching, you are a curious tourist. Walk slowly around to the back of the statue. There you will find a small hole in the pedestal below his back. Insert your key."

Alius looked around and, other than a few cars passing on the street below and a couple kissing on the steps below Lincoln's left foot, there was no one else around. She walked to the back of the statue and there, just above the base, was a narrow slot. She pulled the key from her pocket and inserted it.

A grinding jangle of moving stones shattered the quiet. Surrounding slabs slowly shifted away and the square beneath her feet began to descend beneath the plaza behind the sculpture. Alius pulled the key from the slot and, presently, the stone ground to a halt. She turned on her *orb* and found herself at the midpoint of a long hallway with a door at either end. The positive vectors emanated from her right and, as she approached the entrance, she found a smooth slab of intricately etched stone. She held the *orb* off to the left to cast shadows into the engravings, revealing a huge gathering with every sort of American clapping, cheering, and smiling ecstatically around a fluttering flag.

"Freedom for everyone?" The little *seer* pondered the sheer joy in the scene, *"I wonder what's etched into the other door?"* There was no handle but she found a slot in the center, masked in the flagpole, and inserted her key. The carved slab slid into the wall on her left.

She gazed up at the biggest blue Crystal that she had ever seen. It was several times the size of the one on Morgan's Knot and the magnetic attraction of the energies frightened her, *"I've watched Adrian do this. I know I can do it too!"*

She found the keyhole beneath the spinning Crystal and inserted her key. "Who seeks entry?"

"I am Alius. I am a *seer!*"

The speed of the rotation increased dramatically, the air in the room whistled around in a torrent, and the low rumble of the vibrations overwhelmed the little *seer*. She fought the impulse to flee, until a dark area opened above her, and paused to feel the surging power of the huge gem. *"I can do this!"* She took a deep breath and stepped inside.

A small brilliant blue slab glowed beneath her feet and she felt intimidated by figures crawling all over the inner surface. The voice reappeared, "So you are a *seer!* How may We help you?"

"I've been sent to install a ruby crystal. There is an evil force that is trying to connect all of the dark vectors together to gain absolute power over the world."

"We are aware of your mission and of the disruption in The Balance of the Powers. Before we begin, tell us why you think this monument was built on this particular spot."

"I think it represents the opposition of good and evil, of black and white, of the very best overcoming the very worst in mankind."

"That is very good but there is one more thing…"

Alius thought for a moment, "It represents sacrifice and dedication to defending all that is right and true. President Lincoln didn't pick the easy way but, instead, chose the correct path to bring all of his people together as one nation."

"Ahhh, that was wonderful. We couldn't have said it better."

Alius could almost feel a smile emanating from the energy around her. She waited impatiently, her energy waning.

Finally, the Voice said, "We will generate a target in front of you. Insert the ruby crystal in the center."

Alius pulled the shimmering crimson crystal from her pocket and looked up into a series of brightly colored, concentric circles flashing to an infinite point at the center. They seemed to go on forever and she almost felt that she might fall into the rings but steadied herself, pushing the ruby crystal into the center of the pulsing colors. There was a moment of hesitation before the red stone was sucked into the vortex and disappeared in a blaze of blue.

"You have a great faith in The Balance. We can feel it."

"I had to learn to appreciate The Balance but I am dedicated to its survival."

"As are we all. Your mission is complete. There are four more nodes that have yet to be connected. Time is short."

The dark area opened to her right and she stepped through it, feeling faint and light-headed. The little *seer* stumbled across the floor to lean against a wall for a moment, *"Now I understand what happened to Adrian!"*

The stone door slid back into place, as she stumbled down the hall to the raised plinth at the center. She stepped on the stone and slowly rose to the surface, where she was startled to find the shaft surrounded by police officers pointing guns directly at her.

"Who are you and what were you doing down there?"

"I...I..." The little blond *seer* pursed her lips, they would never understand. The surrounding stones began to move back into position and the officers standing on them scrambled back as the slabs closed around her. There was nowhere to run, so, she stood perfectly still.

Mary's calm voice whispered in her ears. "Concentrate on the tone. See the classroom in the pyramid. You can do this!"

Alius pulled off her glasses, closed her eyes, and was aware of two tones, a deep resonance and the higher, metallic rattle. She focused on the rumbling baritone and saw the six chairs in the classroom. Just as the stones finally scraped back into place, she disappeared.

The policemen were left pointing their weapons at each other. They looked around, bewildered, and holstered their guns. "Where'd she go?"

The sergeant lifted his cap to wipe his brow, "I have no idea and I wish we didn't have to report this. You know someone will want an investigation and how are we going to explain that the stones of the monument opened and a young girl rose up out of the darkness like some diva at the theater...and then disappeared while she was surrounded by, what, a half-dozen armed and highly trained cops?"

"Maybe we should just pretend it was a false alarm!" grunted one of the officers.

"With the way this place is wired, I'm sure it was recorded somewhere."

The younger policeman gazed up at cameras hidden above the statue that surely covered the entire area. "You're right. At the very least, this will take hours to explain in our report."

The sergeant shook his head, snorting, "Make that your report!" and walked away.

Molly, Megan, Morgan, and Kelly parked the wagon on the bluff and skipped down the steps to the beach. It was a warm autumn evening and the water was cool but not cold, as they waded into the surf. The girls swam out beyond the breakers and waited.

Presently, Spot and Dusty surfaced, clicking loudly.

Molly asked, "Have you heard anything about the little subs?"

Dusty swam between the girls, "No, our friends have not found any of them but they are still looking in all of the oceans."

"Ask them to keep searching," injected Megan. "Adrian believes they're out there and it would be helpful to know where they're going. He mentioned an Ice Island which probably means that they are close to one of the poles."

Spot replied, "They are looking everywhere and we will know if they find anything. We'll tell Travis when they are located."

Morgan hugged Dusty, "We certainly appreciate your help! We're all worried about Adrian and Alius."

The girls swam with the dolphins for almost an hour and then retraced their steps up the bluff to the wagon in the dark.

"I wish we knew what's happening," commented Morgan, drying her hair with a towel. "Maybe we should visit the Professor and find out what he knows?"

"I think Dad would have told us if there was anything bad happening but, I agree, let's go to the observatory," said Megan.

"I worry about Adrian and Alius," moaned Kelly. "I know they'll be alright but what if something went wrong?"

Megan turned the wagon north and, thirty minutes later, they marched up the steps to tap the knocker on the Professor's door. Ester opened the weathered oak slab and escorted the girls into the parlor, where Nanchez and Ponte were glued to a *messenger* that was split into two windows. The one on the left showed Gabrielle, Dadeus, Mary, Raffe, and Adrian, who seemed to be staring slightly to the left. The right half of the image showed the faces of several policemen pointing guns directly at the screen.

"That's Alius' point of view," said Ponte nervously, pointing. "It seems they want to know what she's doing, rising up out of the Lincoln Memorial at this hour of the night."

A moment later, the image disappeared, as Alius removed her glasses. The group in the other part of the screen suddenly dashed through a door leaving Dadeus leaning back in his chair with a broad smile.

"She's on her way back," said Ester reassuringly. "They've gone to meet her."

The girls sighed together. "What's happening," asked Kelly.

"Adrian, Alius, and Raffe are moving around the world on the vectors. They've installed ruby crystals in three of the nodes and have four to go to connect all of the positive vectors together."

"I wish I could help," said Kelly quietly.

"Did you talk with Dusty and Spot?" asked Ponte.

"Yes, we just came from swimming with them. They haven't heard anything yet but they said that the sea creatures are looking for the little subs all over the world."

"Then you are helping," smiled Ester.

Chapter 22

Gabrielle, Mary, Adrian, and Raffe waited impatiently, as Alius materialized in the classroom beneath the pyramid, then engulfed her with a big hug.

"Well done!" smiled Adrian. "Three down and four to go!"

Alius grinned and sat down on one of the chairs, "I was feeling pretty positive about what we're doing until I found myself staring down the barrel of a gun…a bunch of guns! That was scary!"

Gabrielle and Mary followed the *seers* into the chamber. "Dadeus is working with Ponte and Nanchez to tap into the vectors through the nodes that you've visited. The power in the system seems to be increasing."

"You've been moving around the globe for hours. Are you hungry?"

"Famished," replied Raffe with a smile.

"Then let's go to the dining dome and have a meal. We can talk about where you'll be going next."

"I keep feeling my energy level going up and down. When we're traveling on the vectors, it seems to increase my strength but entering the Crystals drains it away. I feel as if I've been pulled in both directions," said Alius.

She walked over to Mary and put an arm around her waist, "Thanks for talking me through that scene with the policemen. I wasn't sure what to do!"

"You did fine," smiled Mary. "Have confidence in your powers. You're going to be an exceptional *seer* but you must remember that there is always another way. Be open to what's happening around you, as well as all the options that are available."

Adrian turned to his fellow *seers*, "Did you notice that the tone is almost musical. It seems to rise and fall in some weird soothing rhythm?"

"I didn't notice that so much as another tone, a higher, sort of whiny buzz," said Alius. "It's the same sound I heard while I was studying the Book of Knowledge in the mountain on Morgan's Knot. I always thought it was inside my head or the lighting in the room but it's gotta be the dark vectors!"

"I heard that too! It was very loud when I was near the node," added Raffe.

"Yeah, you're right," replied Alius. "Let's all pay attention to the sounds as we move along the vectors and while we're near the nodes."

"Okay," said the boys together.

They walked through the tunnels and Adrian scurried to catch up with Gabrielle, "I've been so busy with the vectors and the nodes that I forgot to ask how the gardens are growing?"

Gabrielle's eyes crinkled up, "As you will see, our diet has expanded dramatically. We're already getting lettuce, spinach, baby squash, carrots, young onions, beans, and many other vegetables. The fields have all been planted and we're harvesting something every day. George showed us how to use the vectors to accelerate the growing patterns of the plants and the results are rather amazing."

"I know what you mean. Every time that I walk out of The House of the Four Seasons, it seems as if the garden's grown a foot and something new is always ready for harvest. It's one of the blessings of The Balance."

"I agree," said Gabrielle, as they entered the dome. "Let's sit over there, by the windows."

They all trouped to a table and sat together in the curve of the glass sphere. Mesmerized by the divers inserting giant clear panels in the new dome, Alius moaned, "I really want to learn to dive like that!"

"Well, perhaps, when we've finished connecting the nodes, we can make time to fit you for a suit and to teach you the basics," replied Mary. "It really is a magical world."

"One that I'd like to get to know better," giggled Alius.

"Perhaps we should decide on the next set of nodes," Gabrielle interrupted. "I think that we should leave the one in South America until last, as we know something about the others but very little about that one."

A waiter brought their meals and Adrian was amazed at the change. The dishes that had been made from plankton and sea grasses were delicious but now the plates were covered with colorful vegetables and bread made from the first grains grown on the surface.

Dadeus looked concerned, as he walked across the room and pulled up a chair, "I've been talking with Ponte and Nanchez and the connections seem to be functioning. Unfortunately, whoever is building the web of dark vectors is still ahead of us. They seem to be working their way through Europe into Asia," he sighed. "The storm is approaching Jamaica but it hasn't made landfall yet, so we still have a chance to stop it."

Everyone gobbled their meals.

Gabrielle sat back in his chair, "I think that Alius should go to Beijing. Raffe, you take Stonehenge, and Adrian you will go to Jerusalem."

The three *seers* nodded and cleared their plates.

"Raffe, you probably don't know much about Stonehenge. It's a curious structure, in western England, with massive stones set in a circle. It is believed that it was built for spiritual ceremonies, to track the stars and the planets, and it probably served as a calendar. No one is really sure who constructed the monument or when. It has long been believed that the Druids, an ancient tribe, built the structure that stands there now but recent research suggests that earlier structures were started several thousand years earlier. It is certainly a place of great energy and I'm not particularly surprised to learn that it is the site of a node."

"How will I know where to go?" asked Raffe.

"Our research indicates that the most powerful stones are on the northeast side of the structure. They might have been used to mark the point of the rising sun on the solstice. There are several upright blocks with a cap piece across the top and I'd bet that you might find two entrances, one positive and the other negative."

"I'm hoping that there are no slugs lurking about!"

"That was fairly gross," giggled Alius.

"You have no idea!" laughed Raffe. "And the smell was really gross."

"Alius, you'll go to the very heart of Beijing. The Forbidden City was constructed as the center of power for the Ming Dynasty during the early 1400's. It was a city within a city, walled off from the rest of the empire, and history books suggest that there are 9,999 buildings within massive walls built by more than a million workers, many of whom died in the process. The emperor was viewed, not only, as the leader of the nation but as a god."

"The compound is divided into two parts. The public area or the Outer Court, where the emperor's eunuchs exercised absolute control over governmental and domestic matters, is to the south. To the north is the private area where the royal family lived and ultimate power radiated out across the empire."

"The vectors point to a small building in the residential area that was used exclusively by the emperor for prayer and meditation. The node is located beneath that structure. We will guide you to it."

"China is no longer ruled by an emperor. It's a military state," said Alius. "Will I have to worry about guards and guns again?"

Mary smiled, "It is only open to the public during the day, so we'll have to hope that there won't be too many sentries on patrol during the middle of the night."

"I sure hope so. That was scary!"

Gabrielle turned to Adrian, "You'll have the most dangerous assignment. The city of Jerusalem is the spiritual center for the Jews,

Christians, and Muslims. The Christians believe that Christ died, was buried, and arose from the dead in Jerusalem. The Muslims believe that Mohammed rose into heaven, talked with God, and returned to spread the religion of Islam across the known world. To the Jews, not only is it the genesis of the history of their religion, but, now, it is also the bloodied soul of the Promised Land that must be defended."

"Over the centuries, countless wars and battles have been fought for control of the city. Invaders have come and gone but, even today, there's a constant struggle between the Jewish state of Israel and the Muslim residents of Palestine with a Christian community caught in between. It is a dangerous place."

"After visiting the Vatican, I've learned respect and tolerance for each person's right to believe and worship whatever they find in their hearts. I guess I just felt that it was a place where people go, seeking the answers to life's questions, and, if they find what they're looking for, then who am I to judge?"

"That's a very mature point of view," said Mary, with a knowing smile.

"It's a magnificent church and I could feel the power that draws the faithful when I first landed on that marble floor. No wonder people from all parts of the world go there to worship."

"Getting back to Jerusalem, at the center of the conflicting claims is the Temple Mount, where the Muslims believe that Mohammed rose up into heaven. They built a beautiful mosque with a golden dome on top of the ruins of the first Jewish Temple. The only remaining part of that original structure is a wall, which is called the Wailing Wall or the Western Wall. This is a flashpoint where conflicted religions and civilizations collide and a site where confrontations have started over and over again. We believe that the entrance that you are looking for is in the Wailing Wall."

"That makes me feel confident," smirked Adrian.

Dadeus interrupted, "If Alius is heading east, we should get started. Dawn will be coming soon."

Everyone walked back to the pyramid. Dadeus supplied three ruby crystals and left to return to his work on the vectors.

The three *seers* hugged and, with a whoosh, Alius vaporized.

Chapter 23

The little blond *seer* stood very still, listening. A soft breeze tousled her white hair about her face, as she gazed at the moon just rising above the gilded curve of a roof to the east. The heart of the empire was silent, save the chirping of crickets and frogs soothed by water bubbling over stones in a tiny stream flowing through a beautiful little garden. Miles of massive red walls wrapped the grounds but the Emperor's Court was further defended by a moat surrounding another barrier protecting the inner sanctum. The little blond *seer* hesitated for a moment to consider that, through a very long history, an entire civilization viewed this palace as the center of the universe, the spring from which all power and wisdom flowed.

She pulled the glasses from her pocket, put them on, and touched the arms to turn on the audio and video. Looking up towards the sky, the vectors swirled like writhing snakes over the whole area. She flipped the cowl of her robes over her head and stepped from the shadows, walking slowly, quietly along a winding path behind a large red pavilion capped with yellow tiles.

"Yellow or gold, the color of the sun, represented the exalted status of the royal family," said Gabrielle quietly. "The emperor's meditation house is beyond this building, in smaller private garden. Follow the path around to the left."

Alius could feel relentless power radiating through this city within a city with the force of a mighty river meandering through a delta. She wondered whether the citizens, in ancient times, had been in awe of the sheer size of this place because it made her feel small and humble. Every structure was graced with intricately carved appointments, every plant was perfectly groomed, and the gravel beds, surrounding the steppingstones, were raked to appear like flowing water.

Presently, she spotted a tiny red cottage with golden tiles encrusted on the pointed roof like the scales on the tail of some great serpent. It was surrounded on all eight sides by tall, slender trees and there was a burbling moat around the pavilion with a little bridge connecting the tiny island to the path, creating a sense of great privacy. The vectors writhed around the little building, vibrating and crackling in a maniacal dance. "I think I've found it."

"Right you are," said Dadeus. "There's an entrance on the right side."

Alius crossed the humpbacked bridge, protected by fierce dragons carved into the railing, around to the right, and up the steps. The red door was adorned with an intricately embossed sun rising beyond distant mountains, a symbol of the wisdom of his ancestors emerging from the lessons of the past, perhaps? She wondered what the Emperors thought, as they entered through the door of this, their most private and personal sanctum, with the fate of the Empire subject to their meditations. She touched the door with two fingers and it swung away from her with a gentle groan.

As soon as she crossed the threshold, she realized that the room was alive with vectors, spinning and swaying. *"No wonder they chose this spot to build the emperor's meditation pavilion."*

A large ornate throne with a small kneeling pillow dominated the center of the tiny room but the walls were unnaturally plain. There were no carvings to distract from the business of meditation. The little blond *seer* lit her *orb* and scanned the walls and the tiled floor but there was no slot for her key. Frustrated, she perched on the throne.

Alius felt caged in an electric cocoon at the center of vectors swirling around in a dizzying snarl. The whole room shuddered and moaned as the throne began to descend into the floor. She grabbed the arms of the chair and curled into the cushions.

The platform groaned and grumbled and, finally, bumped to a stop. Sweeping her *orb* across hundreds of figures, she realized that the throne was surrounded by a battalion of heavily armed soldiers. They were all facing away from her. The little *seer* stood and walked up and touched the back of one of the guards. It was a perfect stone replica of an intimidating soldier ready for battle!

She held the *orb* above her head and slowly turned around in a circle. The formation stretched for hundreds of feet in every direction, thousands of soldiers, horses, and chariots ready for battle.

"They were placed there to protect the emperor," said Mary. "If these are like other excavations, each one is an individual. No two are alike."

"This is unbelievable," gasped Alius. "He had an army to protect him from his enemies, in life, and this army to protect him from the displeasure of the gods!"

"Do you see the Crystals?"

Alius flicked off her *orb* and followed the vectors careening away to a soft golden glow shimmering on her left. She walked between the soldiers until she could see the giant Golden Crystal spinning rapidly, several hundred feet away. Lighting her *orb*, again, she peered to her right and caught the crackling reflection glistening off the Black Crystal, an equal distance in the other direction.

"The Emperor had both influences in one room," whispered Alius. "The power of this place is overwhelming. I can feel the energy pulling from both gemstones and I know the Emperors had to feel the same charges when they were trying to make decisions. Surrounded by this army, they must have felt invincible and protected, even in the bleakest times. This place is the dark and the light, the kind and the cruel, the good and the evil...all pulling in different directions at the same time."

"Perhaps they could control the intensity during their time, but, whatever their secret, you're probably right in your observations. The Emperors could choose either influence and feel justified in their actions," commented Gabrielle, softly. "It's time to move!"

Slowly, carefully, she edged her way between the statues. Mary was right. Each figure had a different face and an individual stance.

Some carried spears, others swords, and many wore helmets and shields on their arms. She bumped a tall, muscular figure on her right and almost felt that she should apologize. The eyes staring down at her looked fierce and ready for a fight, the figures so lifelike that she felt as if she was moving through a crowd of warriors frozen in place.

Finally, she pressed through the front line to the Golden Crystal. It seemed even larger than the one at Lincoln's Memorial. She knelt to clear the glittering dunes of gold dust beneath the stone and inserted her key.

"Who seeks entry?" The voice echoed throughout the room and Alius turned to look back across the battalion of soldiers. Those on her side of the throne were all leaning, anticipating the command to attack.

"I am Alius and I am a *seer*!"

The speed of the rotation increased, the dark patch appeared, and she stepped onto the small space on the bottom. The globe appeared and the continents broke apart. She studied the glowing dots, scattered across the surface, and zeroed in on an isolated pair of Crystals in the South Atlantic. *"Ice Island"*, she thought. *"I've found it!"*

The voice boomed, "You are here to install a ruby crystal to bind the light vectors together in an effort to stop an evil power that is trying to connect all of the dark vectors!"

Alius was dumbfounded. "That is correct!"

The concentric circles appeared and pulsed away to infinity. The little *seer* drew the ruby crystal from her pouch and pushed it into the center of the smallest ring. She felt a little tug and let go. The ruby crystal flashed away from her hand.

"Your mission is complete and you must hurry. We sense the strength of the dark vectors. Unfortunately, the final node will require great expertise to complete the link. Be cautious."

Alius hesitated for a moment. She could feel her energy draining away, yet she knew that there were two more questions that she must ask. "I noticed a pair of Crystals on an island in the South Atlantic. Is that where the dark vectors are being connected?"

"Yes."

"Would it be better if three *seers* made the link in the final node?"

"You will need all the strength and wisdom that you possess."

"Thank you."

The dark area spread on her right and she stumbled through it. Steadying herself, she felt a trembling wave roll through the cavern and looked across to the throne. The soldiers were moving. Was she delirious from her time in the Crystal, seeing a play of the light from the vectors, or were they really writhing?

She put her glasses back on to see the dark and light vectors flailing wildly, battling for domination. Flashes of light and dark erupted throughout the room and Alius ran as fast as she could between hundreds of soldiers skating around the floor, clashing with those around them. Several fell, as she ducked between them, and the sword of one raked across her back. Three stone chariots crashed into each other, as if they were racing into the melee. The horses, pulling the carts, toppled over backwards while others reared up at her. She ducked beneath their hooves only to face a very tall soldier, wielding a sword in each upraised hand and falling towards her. Alius hurdled behind pieces of a shattered stallion, as the figure crashed to the floor, and raced through the center of the fracas. The little *seer* dove into the throne, panting in panic, and it began to rise above the grand scuffle surging back and forth between the Crystals.

The ascent was painfully slow and the clatter of the battle deafening. When it finally settled in the house of meditation, Alius rushed outside into the cool night air, gasping for breath, and leaned over the dragon banister on the little bridge to gaze down into the water. It seemed so calm and quiet but she noticed little whitecaps flowing this way and that through the reflections of yellow lanterns on the water, no doubt tremors from the uproar in the chamber below.

Afraid to retrace her steps, she closed her eyes, visualized the classroom in the pyramid, and listened for the tone. Instead of single sound, she heard chords and choruses pulsing around her like mayhem in a demonic orchestra. She covered her ears and clenched her jaw to keep from crying out for quiet.

"Concentrate," said Mary softly. "The tone is buried in the sounds that you are hearing. Make yourself calm and listen."

Alius slowed her breathing and centered her mind on the timbre of the tone. Finally, the pitch coalesced above the rest and she was off.

Chapter 24

Raffe flew through the streaming colors and concentrated on the tone. Adrian was right. The sound rose and fell, like a soft, flowing melody but there was another, louder sound growing in intensity. It dimmed, as he bounced from one vector to the next, and then resumed. There was no other sound to compare with the ominous din produced by the black vectors. It was high and whiny but there was a mechanical vibration clattering deep in the tone. At the very least, it was annoying and he struggled to concentrate on the smooth, deep sound of the positive vectors.

Presently, he crashed like a rag doll on a grassy hill, surrounded by huge pillars. Some of the enormous stones stood mysteriously and majestically, where they had been erected by some ancient people, while others had fallen or been knocked over long ago. *"I wonder how they moved these massive stones to this site and then stood them up and placed capstones on top?"*

Gabrielle's description failed to prepare him for the feeling of this touchstone to a culture that disappeared into history. Raffe sensed shifting energies snaking around his body and walked to the center of the circle to gaze at the starry sky. He paused for a moment to think about so many nights searching the sky when he was a child, wondering whether his parents could see the same stars. He grinned at the thought that the heavens were hidden from the population of the underworld. It was hard to believe how dramatically his universe had changed in the past three months. He captured Adrian, found his parents, chased the pirates off the island, and now he was trying to save a world that he knew little about. *"There is so much to learn."*

The young *seer* turned to face Jupiter, just rising over the eastern horizon. Like a keyhole to the heavens, a line of giant stones, capped by huge horizontal rocks, framed the giant planet. He wondered how the ancient people managed to place these colossal stones so precisely. The thought made him understand Adrian's reaction to the St. Peters and the power of man's belief and ingenuity over the constraints of the world around him.

Raffe put on his glasses and was blinded by golden vectors swirling above the frame and arcing away in every direction. They seemed to pass through the near side of the opening, forming a bundle of glowing fibers that dove beneath the stone on the left, balanced by frenetic shadows dancing on the right.

"Amazing," said Dadeus, through the earphone in Raffe's glasses.

"It's just…beautiful," sighed the boy, "and frightening."

"I would guess that you'll find a slot in the stone on the left," said Dadeus, quietly.

"You wouldn't believe the energy that I'm feeling in this place."

"I think I might," replied Gabrielle.

Raffe walked over to the stone supporting the left side of the arch. He turned and gazed around the other side of the circle, "This place is amazing. I thought you might want to see the rest of it!"

"Thanks," said Mary. "Now get to work!"

Raffe pulled the *orb* from his robes and scanned the inner face of the rock. He found the slot right in front of his nose, inserted the key, and waited. Slowly, a deep vibration trembled from beneath the enormous stone. It was similar to the tone they heard while traveling along the vectors but this sound had more than a single pitch, more like a chorus of voices. He reached to retrieve the key.

The noise grew louder and a wave of light surrounded him like a flame erupting from the soil around his feet. The intensity of the radiance grew until he pulled off his glasses to shield his eyes with his arm.

The world was spinning and the giant stones tilted into the dark sky at bizarre angles. He felt his body being passed by a thousand gentle hands as he tumbled into a chasm that opened in the middle of the archway.

He landed in a heap and glanced to his left, where a Golden Crystal cast a soft glow across an enormous cave. It seemed as large as the circle of stones above. He put his glasses back on and cast the light of his *orb* around the room.

He gasped. At the other end of the chamber, a giant Black Crystal rotated rapidly a foot above the floor, "Looks like they've hooked this one up!"

"I'd agree with that," said Dadeus. "Point your *orb* towards that wall over there. What's that texture?"

Raffe aimed the light across the huge cavern. The wall was carved into stacks of stone shelves that rose up to the ceiling, stories above. Hundreds of human skulls were carefully arranged on each ledge and they were all staring at him. He shivered, "Oh, my…"

"Are those skulls?" asked Mary.

"Yes, thousands…maybe millions of them and they're all staring at me!"

"Relax," said Gabrielle quietly. "This must have been a very sacred burial site."

"That's easy for you to say. You're not here and they aren't looking at you!" whimpered Raffe. "Adrian only had to deal with a strange little man. Alius had policemen with guns and stone soldiers. I get slugs and hordes of dead people!"

Like a soothing rush of fresh air, Mary's voice whispered through the headphones, "Calm down. Now concentrate on the Golden Crystal. Walk over and find the slot."

Raffe tried to settle himself. He was panting like a dog on a hot summer's evening as he brushed the gold dust away from the smooth surface beneath the turning stone and found the slot.

He glanced over his shoulder to be sure that the skulls were not gathering for an assault but the room was calm. He inserted his key and the voice boomed through the huge cavern, "Who seeks to enter the Crystal?"

"I am Raffe. I am a *seer*!"

The Crystal increased the speed of its rotation and the dark spot appeared. Raffe stepped inside and found the familiar figures marching in formation. The globe appeared and the continents split apart. He tried to focus on the glowing dots that appeared here and there across the sphere. *"Each of those is another Crystal and another place where people might be working with them."*

The voice bellowed, "How may We help you?"

"I am here to install a ruby crystal to stop an evil force that is trying to connect all the dark vectors together."

"We are aware of your mission and there can be little doubt that the process of connecting all of the dark vectors is nearing completion. You must hurry."

Raffe pulled the ruby crystal from his robes and held it up. The concentric, electric circles appeared and he thrust the gem into the center of the glowing lights. Without prompting from the Crystal, he let go and the red stone flashed away and disappeared.

"Your mission is complete. Is there anything else that We can help you with?"

"Yes. How close are they to binding all the dark vectors together?"

"If they continue at the present rate, We would guess within a day, two at most."

"Thank you for your help," said Raffe, as he collapsed through the dark opening to his right. He crumbled on the smooth stones beneath the Golden Crystal, feeling weak and dizzy, struggling to focus. Gazing around the room, shimmering lights flickered and danced across the stone floor. He put on his glasses, illuminating the vectors bending and swaying to the sound of a chorus reverberating through the enormous cavern. "I don't believe in ghosts but this is...unbelievable!"

Dadeus hesitated for a moment, "I don't think that you're seeing ghosts. Those are the light and dark vectors interacting with each other and the sound that you are hearing is being causing by their friction.

This is a very dangerous place and I'd suggest that you leave as quickly possible. The struggle for domination has begun!"

Raffe took a deep breath and visualized the grassy hill on the surface. He listened through the dissonant clash of the tones and felt the rush lift him to the center of the circle of stones.

He staggered to the middle of the monument to watch the moon descending toward the opposite side of the circle. He gazed at the stars splattered across the sky and relaxed. *"Why do I get to visit the weird ones?"*

The novice *seer* concentrated on the classroom in the pyramid and, with a whoosh, moved into the vectors.

Adrian pulled the cowl of his blue robes over his head, as he landed on the ancient stones on the plaza beneath the Western Wall. He could hear cracks, like gunshots, in the distance and hunkered down, hugging the pavement.

He slipped on his glasses, feeling dwarfed by huge carved blocks soaring into the night and stretching away to either side. Golden vectors vaulted off a terrace above the wall, cascading down the face of the stones like an iridescent waterfall shimmering in the darkness.

"Any ideas?" he asked softly.

"Try the middle of the flow," said Mary.

Adrian flattened himself to the pavement as a bullet, fired into the air somewhere in the city, landed two or three feet to his left with a ping and a tiny cloud of dust. Couching, he ran into the wave of light to press his body against the stones, drenched by the glowing flow of energy. Scanning the wall, he realized the monumental stones had been carefully quarried and fit but there were cracks and crevices across the entire surface. He moved to the center of the lightfall and ran his fingers across the rough stones. *"Thousands or millions of the faithful have prayed in this place and I have one simple request...help me find the slot."*

There were little pieces of paper stuck in gaps and fissures, prayers left by pilgrims perhaps, and he noticed one that was stuck in the very center of a large stone. Gently pulling the tiny wish from the hole, he carefully placed it in another crack and ran his fingers over the notch. He pulled the key from his robes and inserted it into the dark hollow.

Several large stones rumbled away from the wall and the light of the cascading vectors rushed into the breach, drawing the young *seer* in headfirst, amid the murmur of thousands of quiet prayers. The flow tugged him down through centuries of history, bouncing his body like a floppy Teddy Bear, until he landed flat on his back on solid stone with a thump.

He rolled over and gazed around the narrow tunnel, rubbing the bump on the back of his head. The vectors were rushing horizontally along the walls and ceiling like undulating snakes of light and dark. The intensity of the vibrations was far greater than anything that he had encountered anywhere in the system. He stood up and followed the iridescent streams along the shaft until he came to a colossal chasm.

Two giant Crystals, rotating at an astonishing speed, hung in midair within a few feet of each other, one black and the other golden. The vectors were intertwined around both of the gems and sparks erupted in shimmering showers, where dark and light shafts clashed.

"Are you seeing this?"

"It's an intersection," gasped Dadeus. "No wonder this place has seen so many conflicts through the centuries. I didn't know this was possible!"

"What do I do now?" asked Adrian, afraid to approach the tangle of glowing filaments.

"We know there's a slot beneath the Golden Crystal. Move a bit closer and let's see if we can spot it."

Adrian couched and crawled closer to the snarl of sizzling, snapping tentacles of energy. He laid flat to scan beneath the glowing stone, "I've found it."

He pulled up his hood and slithered along the floor under crackling sparks until he was directly beneath the jewel. There was no luster in the glitter of the gold dust and Adrian wondered whether it was a play of the light of the dark vectors dancing above his head.

His fingers brushed across the slot and he inserted the key. The voice asked, "Who seeks entry?"

Hugging the floor, he shouted, "I am Adrian and I am a *seer*!"

The dark area appeared on the surface of the Golden Crystal, directly between the two rotating stones. The dueling forces of the Crystals squeezed and stretched Adrian's body, the vectors coiled around him like voracious electric vines, but he leapt through the dark threshold in the Golden Crystal and landed, face down in a tangle, on the small plate at the bottom of the swirling giant.

The battered boy strained to his knees, relieved to find the clutch of vectors had vanished. He picked up his glasses and placed them in the pocket of his robes, and by the time he stood up, he was facing the spinning globe. The voice appeared all around him, "How may We help you?"

"I have a ruby crystal. There are people who are trying to tie all the dark vectors together and we're hoping that combining all the nodes of the positive vectors will balance their power.

"As you can see, this Crystal is positioned in tight proximity to our dark twin and our vectors vie for space and power. This is a clash that these two stones have waged since the Earth cooled from flowing molten mantle. We are being overpowered by the change and sense that the intensity of the dark vectors is expanding across the globe. You must hurry."

The concentric circles appeared and Adrian thrust the ruby crystal as far into the opening as he could reach and, after the briefest hesitation, released the red stone. It flashed and disappeared.

"Your mission is accomplished."

Adrian paused for a moment, "I'm a bit hesitant to jump into the tangle of vectors between the two stones."

"If you are truly a *seer*, then you possess the power to free yourself."

He stared at the figures swarming across the inside of the Crystal and reluctantly whispered, "Thank you."

The dark area opened to his right and Adrian paused, to put on his glasses, and jumped through the opening. Before his feet touched the ground, he felt the tug and tear of the vectors, twisting around his body. Each brilliant filament vied with all the others to push or pull him toward or away from the Black Crystal, as if the strands of light possessed a vicious essence of their own.

Mary's calm and soothing voice appeared inside his head, "Stay calm. Relax and don't fight against the forces of the vectors. Close your eyes and listen for the tone.

Adrian closed his eyes, his body flopping helplessly as the forces dragged him back and forth across the cobbles beneath the spinning gems. The two tones soared and collapsed, intertwining around each other like the vectors around his body. He could make out the lower tone at times only to lose it in the rush of the high-pitched whine of the second sound.

"Focus!" said Mary softly.

Adrian concentrated on the stone blocks in the wall and the pavement in front of the opening. He listened for the sound and finally felt himself rushing through space. Instead of zipping into the channel, he felt thousands of fingers tearing at his body, viscous hooks shredding his robes. There was no up or down as he vaulted through wild gyrations along the twisted path of the vectors. His arms and legs flailed through brilliant flashes in every color, interrupted by equally dense depressions, the combination draining every ounce of energy and smudging his focus on the stone surface just outside of the wall.

He landed flat on the ground and recoiled out of the chasm, as the colossal stones scraped closed behind him. The light and dark vectors pulled back into the wall fluttering like millions of gleaming sprites waving a desperate good-bye.

He struggled to hands and knees as floodlights flashed across the plaza. The shaken *seer* peered out from under his cowl but the lights were too bright to see who was yelling from the far end of the square. The clatter of footsteps, many footsteps, charged across the pavement, angry apparitions sprinting directly towards him. His heart was racing and he wanted to slump to the ground.

"*Concentrate!*"

He blocked out the noises and commotion around him, focused the chairs in the classroom in the pyramid, and coughed, "*I will be there!*" A moment after the first guard reached to grab his shoulder, he was riding the thrashing hum of the vectors.

Chapter 25

The Reverend Crosby and The High-Lord Barrett joined eight other Whisperers on a dock in a tiny harbor on the southeast coast of England. It was almost midnight, a cold relentless rain drizzled from churning charcoal clouds, and street lamps cast yellow spatters shimmering across weathered cobblestones along the quay of the deserted port. They walked down the gangplank and boarded a black mini-submarine though a hatch on the deck.

The two men moved forward to the passenger cabin and took seats together. The Captain appeared at the front of the compartment, "Gentlemen, would you please fasten your seatbelts. We shall make one stop at a small harbor on the northern coast of France to pick up another group of ambassadors and then we will proceed to our destination. Our expected travel time is six hours."

He carried ten black pendants suspended from golden chains on two fingers of his left hand. "These black diamonds are a gift from our Dark Lord. For your own protection, you will wear them at all times." He walked down the aisle and handed an exquisitely cut gem to each of his passengers. "An attendant will be with you shortly. If there is anything that you need, please don't hesitate to ask."

The High-Lord Barrett admired the glittering facets of the giant diamond and pulled the golden chain over his head, as he leaned over to The Reverend Crosby, "It would seem that our plan is on schedule. Have you seen the news today?"

"Yes, I have. The hurricane is approaching Jamaica and the news bureaus are reporting that it's the strongest storm of the century. The power of our Master's system seems to be increasing."

"I suspect that the technical experts are nearing completion of the connections. Our time is near."

"Add the disturbances in Jerusalem, the Pope's failing health, bombings in the Near and Far East, the financial scandal in Japan, and the computer problems that are radiating through the United States, and I would say that we are seeing the first symptoms of a terminal illness."

The High-Lord Barrett stroked his goatee and the corners of his pale puffy lips curled into a knowing grin, "Yes, my friend, for the first time in history, the entire world will be ruled by a leader with vision, our Dark Lord!"

"Legio Obscurum," replied the vicar.

Four hours later, after a delicious meal, the cabin resonated with the soft snoring of several of the Whisperers. The only other sound was the incessant 'SSssshhhh' of the air bubble that enveloped the submarine slipping through the sea. Using the same technology as the diving suits from the Island of the Children, the tiny craft flew through the water at an astonishing speed. No other craft in the world could keep up with it.

Suddenly, there was a terrific bump and the bow of the black sub swerved hard to port. The violent blow tossed unstrapped ambassadors sprawling down the aisle. Another thump and another.

"What is that?" grumbled the High-Lord, gripping the arms of his chair.

"I have no idea," replied the Reverend Crosby. "A mechanical problem, perhaps?"

"That felt as if it came from outside the craft!"

"I was told that there is no other submarine capable of catching these machines."

"Well, something is!"

Another thump and a deafening pulse vibrated through the whole ship. Fear was growing among the passengers in the cabin, who began yelling to the crew for reassurance.

It was dark in the depths of the Southern Atlantic. The two whales grinned at each other, as they took turns ramming the little submarine. Although they barely heard the almost silent engines, they detected the unusual movement in the water and set off on a tangent that allowed them to intercept the tiny ship.

Metone had taken the first charge at the speeding craft and, once hit, the sleek submarine slowed to a crawl. Pegus bumped it twice and rested his chin on the foredeck, releasing a call to the rest of their pod to set up a gauntlet, the deep resonance rattling through the ship and everyone inside.

Metone laughed, "You are so cruel my brother! You know that your beautiful baritone is probably deafening inside that can! Let's let them proceed at a much slower pace, so we can follow them to their destination."

The two whales moved to press their bodies against the sides of the craft, interfering with the air bubble yet allowing the sub to move along at a modest speed. Their call was echoed throughout the southern Atlantic and other pods followed their example, debilitating submarines on course for Ice Island.

More than a dozen subs were allowed to reach their destination but the entrance to the underwater cove was sealed by a patient swarm of whales.

Chapter 26

Travis was dangling head down in the engine compartment of one of the trawlers when Spot and Dusty surfaced and started clicking insistently. He pulled himself onto the deck and leaned over the side to greet the two dolphins, "Find anything new?"

"We just received a call from our friends in the southern Atlantic. They've trapped a school of small submarines in an underwater mooring on an icy island. I think we've found the place you were looking for!"

"Oh, that's grand!" smiled Travis. "I'll pass it along to the Professor. Tell your friends to keep those subs from leaving that island."

"We'll send the message," clicked Spot.

Travis climbed up to the bridge to call the Professor but stopped short, grabbing the rail to yell to the dolphins, "Thank you!"

"It is our pleasure!" smiled Dusty. The dolphins disappeared beneath the surface of the water and Travis powered up the *messenger*.

Sir Winston strode up the steps of the podium, where Zepallo was seated in a broad leather chair, surveying the screens.

"Sire, there is a problem. Whoever is connecting the positive vectors is catching up with our efforts. The system is becoming unstable and we are losing power."

"I know. I've been watching the progress," sighed the Dark Lord.

"We must find a way to stop them!"

"We know that there are seven nodes that must be coupled to tie the positive vectors together into a worldwide net. There is one that is common to both systems. I must intercede to ensure that they do not make that final connection."

"You must address The Whisperers before you leave. They are distraught about their journeys on the subs and they want to know how we intend to return them to their homes."

"I will speak to the gathering but I am most disappointed in their lack of pluck. These are the people that we have chosen to rule the world?"

"They cower behind your power, Sire," said Sir Winston quietly.

A few minutes later, The Whisperers filed into the conference room. Each wore a black diamond pendent from a golden chain around their necks, protection from the powers of the Black Crystal that also concealed a video and audio link to master machines that were programmed to observe and record everything. On their previous visit, they had been enthusiastic but orderly. Panicked, they were shouting for someone to explain what happened to the submarines over the past few hours and how they would be returned to their homelands when this meeting was finished.

The crowd grew quiet but did not applaud, as Zepallo materialized in front of the spinning Black Crystal. He raised his hands in greeting and peered out from under the cowl of his black robes.

"My friends, we are very close to connecting all of the dark vectors throughout the entire world. The international news reports our storm on the verge of demolishing Jamaica, the banking system in Japan is disintegrating, and the communications net in the United States is in meltdown. These are only a few of the symptoms of our success."

The crowd did not respond. A voice yelled out from the darkness, "What about the subs?"

The black cowl barely swayed in an almost imperceptible expression of his aggravation, "It is our understanding that the interference was caused by an unusual pod of whales. We hope that they will disperse, now that they don't have the subs to play with anymore."

"That's not very reassuring," yelled another of the ambassadors.

"Should they continue their vigil, we will take appropriate actions and we will keep you apprised of the situation. In the meantime, please make yourselves comfortable. Our facilities offer every amenity that you might need and our attendants will be happy to fulfill your requests."

"There is one more connection that must be made and I will see to that myself. If you will excuse me, I'll return shortly," whispered the Dark Lord, as he bowed his head and disappeared.

The three exhausted *seers* sat with Gabrielle and Mary in the classroom in the very heart of the pyramid. "One more to go," said Gabrielle, stroking his beard.

Alius had been quiet since her return from the Forbidden City, "When I was in the Crystal, I found the Ice Island. It's in the South Atlantic. There were two glowing dots that seemed the only possibility."

"We should have picked up on that. We all looked at the same globe," said Raffe.

"Well, at least we've a place to start looking," commented Mary.

"The Crystal also said that the connection in the final node would require all the wisdom and power that we possess," said Alius softly. "I think we should all go together."

Adrian gazed boggle-eyed from fatigue, "I agree. We know this node is the odd one and we have no idea what we'll find when we get there."

"It can't be any weirder than what we've all been through to get this done," mumbled Raffe.

Gabrielle said, "One for all and all for one?"

The three *seers* grinned and roused a little.

He continued, "We've seen the dark and light vectors thrashing about in the areas around the last nodes that were connected. I'd guess that our efforts are producing a disruption in the flow of energy through the dark vectors. We should consult with Dadeus before you leave on your final journey."

With that thought, the old Keeper rushed into the classroom, "I've just heard from Ponte. The whales have found the mini-subs and followed them to an island in the South Atlantic. They have the subs trapped in an underwater harbor and I've located it on our equipment."

Everyone grinned at Alius, who blushed. "Alius already told us where the island was located but that's terrific," said Mary. "We were just talking about the final connection. Do you have anything that you want to add?"

Dadeus pulled up a chair, "The instruments indicate that the vectors are becoming more violent. The scenes that we saw in your last three stops suggest the two systems are brawling with each other for dominance. If we can make the final connection, I think we'll have a chance to thwart their efforts. When both systems are completed, there will be a balance of sorts."

"What about the final node?" asked Adrian.

"We have no information on which to base a theory. The region's history is interesting," he paused. "There is an ancient sacred city called Machu Picchu, built by the Incas high in the mountains to the south of the area where these particular Crystals are located and there are huge drawings in the desert called Nazca lines that depict animals and men, from some prehistoric time, trying to send a message to the gods in the sky. Neither of these sites seems to be tied directly to the twin stones because it seems that this node was too remote to become established as a center-point of spiritual understanding by the many cultures who thrived in the area over the centuries. In spite of the tangled web of light and dark arrays spewing from this site, they used the powers of these vectors but probably never traced them to their source or, for that matter, if they did, the snarl of energies around these stones might have frightened them off. I can't know for certain but I would guess that the two Crystals are very close together in a never-ending tug of war, which would explain why no one ever succeeded in harnessing the Powers directly. This pair could be very dangerous."

The three *seers* glanced at each other nervously until, finally, Adrian whispered, "It always seems to reach this point, where there is no other choice but to move forward." He rubbed his eyes and struggled to stand, "Let's go find the final node."

Dadeus handed a ruby Crystal to Adrian, who placed it in his pocket, "I have something else that I would like you to take along on this mission. He pulled three golden rings, molded around large amber crystals, from the pocket of his robes and held them up to the youngsters.

"We do not believe in weapons and I have to admit that I am embarrassed that I developed these. I originally thought of using them against the pirates but, fortunately, Adrian found a better way."

He put one of the rings on his right hand and pointed it at the wall on the other side of the chamber. The Keeper squeezed his fingers together and a bolt of lightning blew a gaping hole in the fitted stones with a tremendous boom. Dadeus smiled sheepishly as he pulled the ring from his finger, "This is probably the largest, so you take it, Raffe."

"Cool!"

The Keeper's smile disappeared as he handed a ring to Adrian and Alius, "Don't use these unless you have to. They're certainly capable of great destruction and would take the life of a man easily. I'd rather you found a better way…again."

The three *seers* slipped the rings on their fingers, joined hands, and stood in a circle. "After you leave, I'll call Ponte to let him know what's happening. Is there anything that you want me to pass along?"

Adrian thought for a moment, "Yes, there is. Would you ask the Professor to ask the girls to talk with the dolphins, Spot and Dusty. Tell them where we're going and ask them to send the message to all of the animals in the region. We're gonna need their help!"

"I'll tell Ponte. Now, you're aiming for a cave or hollow at the base of a jagged cliff at the edge of the jungle. The power of the vectors suggests that this one is fairly close the surface. Be careful."

"Are we ready?" asked Raffe.

Adrian and Alius nodded and listened for the deep rumble of the tone. A moment later, the *seers* were ricocheting along a vector, the colors and blobs of darkness coursing past in a blinding rush. They struggled to maintain focus on the destination and each other through the roughest journey that any of them had endured. The timbre was just barely distinguishable from the blaring chorus swirling around the tumbling vibrations.

They clutched each other desperately, rebounding through one flashpoint after another until they landed on slippery rocks and tumbled to the bottom of a deep ravine. Wings of stone jutted out from the sides of the mountain framing narrow jagged crevices plunging hundreds of feet back into the rock.

The three *seers* donned their glasses and clamored up the craggy cliff. All of the vectors erupted from a dark crevice between two massive outcroppings, enormous electric snakes wriggling out of a burrow to arc across the sky in all directions. Glowing bundles were spinning in the air above their heads like a child's top wobbling out of control and dark vectors intertwined with the golden strands coiling into a pulsing tornado of energy. Violent flashes spewed splatters of sparks where the light and dark intersected.

They started to ease closer to the vector point when a flash erupted from the darkness and the ground exploded around their feet. They crouched, rings extended to a tall figure in dark robes that barely brushed shiny boots. He wore a deep cowl to conceal his face and held his left hand out with a silver band bearing a large black diamond on his ring finger.

"Zepallo!" yelled Adrian.

The three *seers* crouched closer in panic, joined hands, and trembled together. Raffe whispered, "We could jump back into the vectors."

The Dark Lord pulled the cowl from his head to reveal a smooth, though aging face with pale skin, long dark hair streaked with white, and intense blue eyes...like Adrian's eyes, only cold. His thin lips curled into a sinister smile, "Three young *seers*! Welcome to the real world...my world!"

"You can't defeat us! There are three of us!" shouted Raffe.

"My young man, you might never conceive of the power that I possess. I could have taken you out with my first thrust! You're obviously well trained, though inexperienced, *seers* but I respect your powers just the same. Rather than destroy each other, I might suggest that you join me. I'll teach you things beyond your wildest imaginings."

"I was raised to believe in the powers of the Black Crystals, until I learned about the wonder of The Balance," cried Alius. "I know what you have to offer."

"My dear, you could not possibly know the depth of my knowledge," smiled the dark figure patiently, wagging a long bony finger.

"I've seen both sides. I know the difference. The light is more powerful than the dark."

"You are certainly self-possessed, aren't you? I, too, have been exposed to both the light and the darkness," sighed Zepallo, as he raised his hands above his head. Roiling storm clouds dimmed the sky. Lightning sizzled through the heavens, thunder crashed through the canyon, and torrents of rain fell around the *seers*, sweeping a cascade of rocks down the hill. The downpour transformed into sleet and then giant snowflakes and, when he pointed a finger, the sun reappeared.

The three *seers* squeezed the water from their robes in an awkward attempt to conceal their awe at the powers of the Dark Lord.

"Cool!" said Raffe, as he caught a snowflake in his palm that flashed into a dark dancing flame and evaporated.

Alius jabbed an elbow into his ribs and whispered, "Be afraid. Be very afraid!"

The girls returned to the beach and passed Adrian's message to Spot and Dusty, who asked a pod of whales to broadcast it to the rest of the world. Their ultra-low tones resonate for hundreds, perhaps, thousands of miles and, within minutes, the message passed from one group to the next until it reached a clutch of otters romping in the waters along the western coast of Peru.

They surfaced and the call went out to a cluster of lazy sea lions, basking in the sun on the rocks along the shore. Seagulls, flitting above the breakers, broadcast it along the animal network. Within minutes, every creature in the northern half of the country was searching for the three *seers*.

A giant condor soared along a rocky slope where tiny rivulets of water seeped from fissures dribbling into tiny pools overflowing into a babbling brook that irrigated an immense forest stretching to the Atlantic. The remaining flow cascaded down into valleys, merging with other streams into the mightiest river on the planet. The world's largest vulture was searching for the dead or dying who might be exposed near fresh water but even the living were still and unmoving.

He heard the message being passed throughout the mountains but was surprised to spot three young people dressed in blue robes standing close together just outside a deep crevice in the rock. He tucked his feathers close to his body and dropped out of the sky. At the last moment, he extended massive wings and swept just above their heads. The vulture was startled to see another figure standing in the shadows, a tall man dressed in black robes, a dangerous man surrounded by an aura that churned like storm clouds at night and sizzled with the darkest of energies.

The huge bird soared above the mountain and called to his mate, circling several hundred feet above the humans on the rocks. Suddenly a flash of lightning and peels of thunder rippled around the peaks. Clouds blocked the sun, rain fell, then sleet and snow before the tiny tempest dissipated. The female rose up and screeched. The message passed from one bird to another and then to the animals who lived throughout the forest. The reaction was instantaneous.

Simian and Sammy huddled with more than forty members of their family in the cavern with the giant Green Crystal, which was rotating at an incredible rate.

The storm was hovering just off the southeastern coast of Jamaica and had not moved in hours. The island was buffeted by thunderstorms and high winds surging from the northeast but, so far, the damage was minimal compared to reports from Kingston and Ocho Rios.

Mothers reassured crying children, sitting on stone pews in the green glow of the spinning stone, waiting for some word on the progress of the storm over a tiny transistor radio. Everyone pitched in to board up homes and shops and the market had been completely cleared, transforming the cultural center of the entire community into a huge empty parking lot. Provisions had been stockpiled in the cave to last for days and several women were working on the next meal.

Sammy noticed Simian sitting on the base of the Alter in front of the Crystal. His eyes were closed and his breathing very shallow, as if he were meditating. He walked over to sit next to his uncle, whispering, "Are you alright?"

"Yes, I'm fine. I'm feeling a disturbance in the vectors."

"That doesn't surprise me. Wasn't this storm created through the vectors?"

"Yes, but this is a different disturbance. It is more like a confrontation of powers and it's not too far away," whispered Simian, his eyes remained closed.

"Is there anything I can do?"

"No, but I think that there is something that I must do. Our friends need some help. Take care of the family, you'll be safe here. I'll be back when I've finished." Simian took a deep breath and disappeared.

Mary, Gabrielle, and Dadeus crowded around the monitors, watching three simultaneous views of Zepallo. "I can't stand this!" cried Mary. "I have to go to help them!"

"Are you sure that you're capable of riding the vectors? You've only had one lesson and the vectors are behaving badly!" implored Gabrielle.

"If our young *seers* can do this, then I must too!" said Mary, very softly. She closed her eyes, focused on her young charges, and listened for the tone. The precise pitch was encased in the dissonant noise of clashing vectors and it took persistent concentration before she heard the rumble. A moment later, she was gone.

Mary felt as if she was being drawn and quartered by the snarl of vectors. The colors blurred in a dizzying rush through globs of darkness and she struggled to maintain her concentration as the first flash of brilliant light blurred her vision when she bounced through a node. *"Concentrate! If they can do this, then I can too."*

After several more flashpoints, she landed on the ledge within a few feet of the three children, followed by Simian who appeared like a mirage beside her. The young *seers* pulled off their glasses to greet their friends and the elders closed behind them. "Now we are five," said Mary. "Believe in the Balance and all that you know to be true. He has no power over truth!"

Zepallo smiled, "There are more of you! Have you invited even more guests? Shall we have lunch catered in?"

"I think five of us will be enough," cried Adrian.

"Well, being a good host, the very least I can do is to repeat my offer for your friends. I've asked these young people to join with me to form the most powerful force on the face of the Earth. I would like to extend that invitation to you two, too!"

"You know we'll not accept your offer," said Simian. "We believe!"

Under his breath, Simian murmured, "Do you see his aura?" The other *seers* turned to the man in the black robes. He continued, "Squint you eyes a little and you'll notice that he's surrounded by an egg shaped aura. His is gray."

Everyone focused on Zepallo. "I see it," said Alius.

"Me too," said Raffe. "It's flickering with sparks."

"Each of us has an aura, which reflects the energies that we project but it can also provide protection. If you focus just a foot or so in front of us, you'll see that our auras have joined together, like an invisible bubble surrounding us. Ours is golden," smiled Simian.

Again, the other *seers* squinted their eyes. "I see it," said Adrian. "It shimmers like looking through a waterfall into sunlight."

"That's it. Our powers have merged together. Have faith in your beliefs because that is what this battle is about, is it going to be a golden world or a future dominated by his demonic forces?"

"We appreciate your offer but we came to connect the final node!" yelled Adrian, as a tiny hummingbird fluttered around his head and peeped in his ear, "Help is coming!"

Brigades of ants crawled from the fractures in the rocks, then slugs, snails, spiders, cockroaches, grasshoppers, crickets and a smorgasbord of birds lined the rocks above the ledge. The insects were followed by waves of small snakes, lizards, mice, and rats. A flurry of bats fluttered out of the shadows, spinning around the Dark Lord like a whirling storm.

"As you like," sighed the Dark Lord, lifting his left hand to the five *seers*.

Adrian, Alius, and Raffe raised their fists and aimed their rings at their foe. Before anyone could fire a blast, a menagerie of animals of every description surrounded the five *seers*. Puma, jaguar, deer, goats, cows, llama, turtles, horses and ponies, rabbits, squirrels, fox, skunk, bears, bore, and wild dogs gathered close. Toucan and macaw led thousands of birds of every imaginable hue, and an incredible swarm of flying insects hovered over their heads. Butterflies in outrageous colors fluttered around their faces. The herd of animals absorbed the *seers* and started edging forward.

As the first wave of insects reached Zepallo, a hawk plowed through the cloud of bats with talons extended to clench his black cloak, screeching as he pecked at face and eyes. The Evil One shrieked in pain and an errant blast from his ring shattered the rock face of the outcropping to his left.

The hawk fluttered and backed away from the Dark Lord, who wiped the blood from his face and peered out at the throng pressing around him. Ants and spiders were climbing his robes and rats, mice, lizards, and snakes slithered up his pants legs and into his boots to nibble at his feet and ankles. A swarm of flies, mosquitoes, wasps, and bees buzzed around his face and the herd of animals let out a riotous roar.

Zepallo fired another blast from his ring at the five *seers*. The lightning spread into a flaming arc racing across the rocks and bounced over the aura surrounding the herd. The *seers* didn't have time to react to the flash and watched, in awe, as the energy rolled over the entire throng. The golden aura shimmered and danced as the pulse passed and the *seers* returned to face their foe.

There would be no victory against this growing mass of creatures in spite of his many weapons and talents. His body twitched and the long black robes quivered, as insects and animals gnawed up his legs, "Connecting this node will demand more of you than any of the others! Which begs the question of whether any of you play chess?"

Adrian raised his hand.

"Yes, well, I suspect that you are probably a young prodigy, so you will understand that this is merely the opening move of a single pawn in what will prove to be a long and arduous match...unless, of course, you decide to accept my most gracious offer. Whether you are successful or die trying, our work will continue and the dark vectors will be connected." Swatting at the insects around his face, he bowed his head and disappeared.

The *seers* cheered and the animals bellowed. Everyone pressed into the crevice between the huge slices of rock, passing behind a small steaming waterfall into the chamber that confined the two Crystals.

Adrian gasped at his first sighting of the giant spinning stones. The gems were grinding against each other and, where they touched, waves of searing sparks and gleaming gemstones spewed in every direction. The floor beneath the brawling gems was slick with rivulets of molten gold and super-heated diamonds, glowing deep crimson in the dim light, and the rasping racket overwhelmed the senses.

The animals remained at a safe distance, wary of the intense energies, but Adrian was drawn to the raging inferno, a moth to the flame, fascinated by the enigma and terrified of the solution. He covered his ears with his hands and edged around the gnashing Crystals, certainly the largest that he had ever seen.

His glasses revealed the vectors flailing around the Crystals in a tangle of toxic tentacles, gold and gloomy gray. The stones spewed intertwined strands of dark and light vectors out through the ceiling and the whole chamber creaked and shuddered under intense pulses, as the positive and negative energy struggled for supremacy.

He pulled the cowl of his robes over his head and crawled beneath the Golden Crystal, where he scraped the floor with his key until he uncovered the slot buried under a crust of glowing gold and diamond shards. It was lying directly between the two stones. He backed away and returned to the other *seers*.

Mary put her arm around his shoulders and motioned the rest of the group to move outside, where they could talk.

The animals surrounded them, as they moved into the light and Mary said, "This one's different than any of the others that we've worked with. The energies are so knotted that it seems impossible to enter the positive Crystal...and survive."

"Up until now, it's been a game of mind over matter. I'm not sure how to approach this one," sighed Adrian, trying to mask his fear and exhaustion.

Simian almost whispered, "Maybe we can alter The Balance."

"What do you mean?" asked Alius.

"Well, even though it seems that there is a war going on in that chamber, there is also an equilibrium. The two Crystals have been fighting for dominance for millennia but neither is winning. They are destroying each other very slowly."

"That's what it said in the Books, *'Break The Balance',*" added Adrian.

"But how do we tame that brawl?" asked Raffe.

"First, with our faith in the things that we know to be true...The Balance and the power of the Positive Crystals. Look around at all of these animals. They represent the positive in nature. You saw the aura surrounding the evil one and the golden bubble around the five of us. Look at the animals and tell me what you see?"

The other *seers* gazed around at the herd of animals sprawling over the side of the mountain. Their auras merged into a shimmering cloud of amber radiance.

"Oh, my," said Mary. "That is incredible."

"They are an energy source," said Simian simply.

Raffe raised his fist, "We have another energy source. The rings!"

"Right," said Adrian. "I wonder whether we could use all of this energy to disrupt the balance of the two Crystals just long enough to allow me to insert the ruby crystal?"

Simian smiled, "I think you're beginning to see another possibility."

Adrian turned to the animals and held up the ruby crystal, "To save the Balance as we know it, I must insert this ruby crystal in the Golden Crystal in the cave. Would you be willing to help?"

The animals all roared, grunted, barked, hissed, and yowled their approval.

"Alright, we need your positive energy. We'll move into the cave and focus on the Golden Crystal. When I'm ready, the other *seers* will fire the energy from these rings to nudge the stones apart and, hopefully, it will give me enough time."

The animals agreed and everyone marched back into the cave. Adrian felt a bit more secure in the warmth of animals, who packed into the chamber, wavering between the dangers of the spinning stones and the reassuring confidence of the *seers*. He handed his ring to Simian, "Just squeeze your fingers together and it'll go off. Wait until the dark hole appears and then fire away. I'll move as soon as I can."

Simian grabbed his shoulder, "You are a brave and talented *seer*. Are you sure you don't want me to do this?"

"I've done it before and you haven't. I'll be faster,"

"Alright," said Simian, wrapping his arms around Adrian. "Be careful!"

"Just don't shoot me with those rings!" grinned Adrian.

He handed his glasses to Mary, pulled the cowl of his robes over his head, fingered the black diamond pendant around his neck, crept carefully through the shower of sparks and rivers of fiery gold to the space between the two stones, scraped the liquid gold from around the slot, and inserted his key. The soles of his shoes and the front of his tattered robes were smoldering and his body lurched convulsively, as the vectors punched and pulled from every direction. The dark hole slowly erupted in the side of the Golden Crystal, flashing from light to dark, crackling like shattered glass. The voice was distorted by all the energy flying around the room, "Who seeks entry?"

"I am Adrian and I am a *seer*!"

Adrian turned to look around the room. Hundreds of animal faces were gaping at him from the every nook and cranny. He nodded and waited as they started concentrating on the Golden Crystal. The two gems seemed to move slightly apart and Adrian pointed to his fellow *seers*.

Three violent flashes flew across the room and exploded between the two fighting gems above his head. The two stones moved farther apart and he leapt through the breach.

He crouched on the small space, the figures zooming around the interior surface in crazy, haphazard patterns. Here and there, blotches of darkness mushroomed and disappeared in blobs through the intense radiance. The globe appeared and faded, without going through the introductory routine.

A warbling voice asked, "How may We help you?"

"I'm here to install a ruby crystal," replied Adrian. The rushing wind, flickering light, and grinding growl reminded him of the inside of an enormous kitchen blender. The vibration of the small slab beneath his feet tossed him off balance and made his teeth chatter. He felt the energy draining far more quickly than any other visit and he knew that his time was short.

"We have been awaiting your arrival," said the voice.

The electric circles tried to form but they kept dimming in and out of focus. Adrian held the ruby crystal at arm's length, ready for insertion, and waited for the rings to glow brightly.

Suddenly, there was a flash and the rings pulsed rapidly. He thrust the ruby crystal as far as he could reach into the vortex but it would not release and he was pulled in with it. His body flashed through a tornadic kaleidoscope, twirled around in splashes of incredible color with the force of giant ocean waves, before being tossed into another whirlpool of darkness. Sparks flew in every direction and every glimmer of hope was smothered by blobs of gloom. His clutched his ears, hammered by a racket that sounded like the inside of the largest engine on earth in desperate need of lubrication.

The young *seer* curled into a ball plunging through streamers blinking from dark to light and back again. Rapid surges from sizzling heat to a frigid chill scorched his skin and he wondered whether his energies were being torn between the two Crystals because there could be little doubt that pieces of his body were about to fly off in different directions to be incinerated and consumed by the powers. He wanted to scream and opened his mouth but no sound could escape through the raging din. As he hurtled into a gaping darkness, consumed in a hopeless gloom, three golden explosions erupted around his body, flinging him through the dark hole in the Golden Crystal.

Adrian landed squarely on top of the other *seers* and animals, who were crowded in front of the two Crystals. "What happened?" he yelled and then realized that the noise had subsided.

Everyone laughed and dragged him to his feet. He was dizzy and weak, his shredded robes and shoes smoldering, as he sagged between Mary and Simian. The young *seer* glanced over his shoulder to the spinning gems, which were several feet apart and spinning at a normal rate.

"When you did not reappear, we decided to try one more blast and suddenly you popped out of the Golden Crystal like a cork out of a bottle," snickered Simian. Mary, Alius, and Raffe all hugged Adrian and the animals gathered around to offer their congratulations.

"Thank you everyone," said Adrian. "I really didn't think I was going to survive!"

Mary handed him the glasses and said, "Put them on, Dadeus has something that he wants to say."

Adrian slipped the glasses on with trembling fingers and peered around the room. The vectors still snapped and crackled but they were far more calm than before he entered the Crystal.

"Well done, my boy. You've done it! The nodes are all connected."

"I don't think I want to try that one again," stammered Adrian.

"We'll get to work and see what we can do, now that the net is complete," said Dadeus. "I will expect all of you back here immediately!"

"We're on our way," said Adrian. He pulled off the glasses and stuffed them into his pocket. Turning to the animals surrounding the five *seers*, he said, "I want to thank every one of you. Without your help and your energy, we never would have completed this task. You've saved The Balance, as well as my life, and we'll always be in your debt."

A sleek black jaguar moved to the front, his golden eyes glowed with affection. "It is we who should be thanking you. You risked your life for all of us and our way of life. We will send word back through the whale mail to let the natural world know that this threat has passed. All of you are welcome in this forest when you have a chance to return."

The *seers* petted every animal within reach and then joined hands, closing their eyes to concentrate on the tone together. It was suddenly very clear and, a moment later, they disappeared.

Chapter 27

The five *seers* landed back in the classroom in the pyramid and found Gabrielle pacing back and forth between scattered chairs. He smiled as he hugged each of them, "Come along, Dadeus is on the *messenger* with Ponte."

Simian raised a finger, as he gazed at the murals on the walls, "Is this the story of the descendants of Protus?"

Mary put an arm around his shoulder, "Yes, it is. This is where they landed when the fled Jamaica."

"Then we are related," smiled Simian. "The Golden Book told me that I was an heir to his lineage."

Raffe laughed and clapped him on the back, "We're distant cousins! I just found out too."

Gabrielle said, "You are family in this house. Now, if we could move along, the Keepers are waiting."

They moved through the tunnels, with Simian lagging behind in wonder, and trudged up the stairs into the workshop, where Dadeus leaned close to his equipment. A large *messenger* projected Ponte's face. He was smiling and greeted the *seers* as they entered the room, "Welcome back! Well done!"

Dadeus turned from the control panel, "After I talked with you, we realized that the two systems overlap in three places…here, Morgan's Knot, and the node that you just connected. We've decided to send a pulse of energy from the positive vectors through these intersections. Hopefully, it will back up the systems on that Ice Island in the Southern Atlantic.

He turned back to the *messenger*, "Our systems seem to be in sync with each other. On my count, send your pulse. Three, two, one…" As he hit a button on the console, all the lights in the domes dimmed for a few seconds and then returned to normal.

Ponte's face reappeared on the *messenger*, "We'll monitor the network to see if our little experiment worked. We'll get back to you in a little while. Oh, Adrian and Alius, your parents would really like to see you at home as soon as you can manage it!"

Adrian and Alius hugged, "We'll be there shortly!"

The group moved to the dining dome and sat down at a large table for a meal. Simian gazed around at the construction of the dome and the amazing variety of fish swimming outside. "This is fantastic! I want to know everything about everything!"

Gabrielle laughed, "That seems to be the universal reaction lately. I would love to give you the tour."

Soule and Amy stopped by to offer their congratulations and Adrian gave each a big hug. "We've only had a couple of opportunities to use our suits on Morgan's Knot but I think everyone is excited about learning to dive. Would you two come to our Island and teach our friends?"

"We'd be happy to. You just say when!" laughed Amy.

"We're off to give lessons, but we'll see you soon," smiled Soule, as they strolled across the gleaming floor of the dome.

The *seers* joked about their adventures and wondered at the powers in each of the strange situations they encountered.

"I thought I was a goner, when I rose up in the middle of those policemen and all of those guns," laughed Alius.

"Well, that wasn't as bad as a cavern full of giant slugs, which was totally gross!" snorted Raffe. "Then there were those million skulls staring at me! Why'd I get all the weird ones?"

"After facing that stone army, I wonder whether the character of the powers and the influences of the Crystals are unique to each pair?" pondered Alius.

"I had several thoughts along the way," mumbled Adrian. "First, I learned to respect everyone's right to believe as their hearts direct them. The Basilica was awe-inspiring and I'd like to go back there someday, just to have the time to actually appreciate it when I'm not completely petrified. I'd also like to go back to Jerusalem. The powers cascading over the Wailing Wall were amazing and the feeling of standing at a center-point of history was overwhelming. The other thought that keeps nagging at me is that Zepallo said this was merely the opening move. He's out there somewhere and we all know that he's plotting to complete his plan for world domination. We haven't seen the last of him."

"I believe you're right," said Gabrielle solemnly. "We might have balanced the forces but his technicians will complete the web of dark vectors and he'll find another way to fulfill that quest for dominance."

Simian nodded, "He is an evil man who will not give up until he is stopped."

"I'm thinkin' a whole bunch of us," said Raffe. "That was one bad dude and I sure wouldn't want to face him alone."

"We are stronger when we are united," said Simian.

"Amen to that," added Mary.

Despite giddy exhaustion and relief in surviving their missions, each of the *seers* was quiet through the rest of the meal, as they contemplated Zepallo's frightening powers and a future charged by his warning. As they finished, Mary turned to Alius and said, "You said that you wanted to learn to dive. How would you feel about getting scanned for a suit?"

"Really?" smiled Alius, "Let's go!"

Mary laughed as they stood to leave, "Now that I know how to ride the vectors, I'll bring it to you when it's ready!"

Adrian leaned back in his chair, "I'd be happy to teach her the basics but there's still so much that I want to learn from Soule and Amy. We'll have to come back or, better yet, have them come to Morgan's Knot to teach our people."

"That will be arranged," said Gabrielle.

"My mother has been collecting the materials to start producing the suits, so maybe we'll be ready for a visit soon."

Gabrielle pressed a knuckle to his lips, "I just want you to know how proud and thankful we are, of all of you, for your bravery and dedication to The Balance. Working together has made all of us stronger and more secure. I believe we can be certain that we will face other obstacles and enemies in the future but, in the meantime, I think it would be wise to have all of the *seers* searching the Texts for references to other people who are working with the Crystals. That is our next challenge…uniting our forces."

"We know that Zepallo will appear again and I'm pretty sure he's got an army behind him," said Adrian quietly. "Having more groups working against him might help the next time."

"I agree, having the technology and expertise to bind the dark vectors together would require vast manpower and resources," sighed Gabrielle. "Is there anything else that we need to cover before you leave?"

"Yes, there is," said Adrian. "I'd love to see what you're doing on the plaza. I noticed some construction, the new stone stacked up, and mason's tools lying about."

"We'd love to show you the progress that we've made," laughed the old man. His beard swayed back and forth as he rose from his chair, "Let's go!"

The group filed through the tunnels and emerged from the entrance under the waterfall. The sun was high in the sky and Adrian had no idea of how many days or weeks passed since he and Alius left Morgan's Knot.

They traced the path through the jungle to the plaza under long shadows creeping across the white stones. Birds fluttered around them and a pair of spotted panthers strolled out of the jungle with a trio of romping kittens. An elephant drove pallets of stone from one spot to another and several monkeys whisked up gravel and stone chips left by the masons.

Adrian surveyed the buildings surrounding the square and many were beginning to reveal their former splendor. Walls were being reconstructed behind columns growing before the row of buildings, forming a colonnade. "It seems that you've plenty of animal help on your project!"

"Without their assistance, we couldn't have accomplished even a fraction of this. In fact, they volunteered. When the first load of stone arrived, the elephants met the boat and unloaded pallets of stone without breaking anything. They work without much instruction and just seem to know what's going to be needed and organize themselves," said Gabrielle.

Simian turned around and around, "There are drawings on the walls of the cave, where the mighty Green Crystal turns, that look just like this."

"Perhaps they would have built our little city in Jamaica if they hadn't been scared off by the white devils," replied Raffe.

Simian smiled, "I think you're right."

Gabrielle produced a scroll of the final plan and rolled it out for his guests. "Although the history books suggest that certain tribes within the Mayan culture performed sacrifices on the mainland, we found no evidence of those practices here. Rather, they seem to have used several of these structures as temples for worship and the largest, at the end of the plaza, was undoubtedly a library. The plaza was their gathering place. They stored their foods in cellars beneath some of the buildings and used others for social, spiritual, and intellectual pursuits. Everything happened around this square."

Adrian gazed around the tiny city that was rising out of the jungle just as it had when those first refugees arrived from the mainland to protect their culture and their beliefs. Lacy ferns waved from the shadows and bright red hibiscus and snowy gardenia bloomed in the open areas between the buildings. Spaces had been left for planting more trees and shrubs when the construction was completed. "It must have been magnificent when it was first built and it will be just as beautiful when you've finished."

As they wandered from one building to the next, Alius and Mary materialized, giggling like schoolgirls.

"We plan to use the pyramid as our classroom but we hope to fill the library with books and texts that cover the entire history of the powers," commented Mary. "My hope is that it will become a miniature version of the library in Alexandria!"

"That's a worthy goal," smiled Alius, "and a good place for Raffe to study the Egyptians!"

Raffe blushed and grinned, "After the places we've visited, I've realized how much there is to learn about the people of our world. No matter how much we discover, there will always be more!"

"Sort of like the Texts and the Crystals," smirked Adrian.

An hour later, they hugged in the classroom and Raffe said, "We'll come to visit you. I want to see Morgan's Knot!"

"Anytime," said Adrian.

Simian handed the ring to Adrian and wrapped his arm around the boy's shoulders, "You were very brave to enter those spinning monsters and I think that we've all learned some valuable lessons."

"I believed in all of you," said Adrian. "The Light is more powerful than the Darkness."

The little Jamaican's white teeth glistened when he smiled, "I will come back to Morgan's Knot when we have finished cleaning up after the storm. Until then, take care of yourselves." With that, he closed his eyes and vanished.

Mary hugged Alius, "I promise, I'll bring your suit to you as soon as it's ready. I want to see Morgan's Knot too and, perhaps, I can help Sara with training the tailors to produce the suits."

Adrian and Alius thanked their friends, joined hands, and disappeared.

Chapter 28

After dinner, an exhausted Adrian followed his mother out through the kitchen door to sit on the steps. He found it amazing that it was only months ago they sat together under the stars and he worried about spending a couple of months with George and Elsie. It seemed another lifetime.

His mother pulled her son close, "I'm very proud of all that you've become since we sat here, what four months ago?"

Adrian smiled, "Two minds, one thought. I was just thinking about that night. I was scared that you and Dad would sail away on the Sparrow and I'd never see you again."

"It seems that it was for the best," sighed his mother, scanning his ragged robes. "From the looks of you, I'd guess you had quite an adventure. You know every time you do these marvelous things, I feel I age at least a decade!"

They laughed together. It was good to be home.

"School's already started and you can begin classes on Monday," smiled his mother, ruffling his blond waves. "And you still need a haircut!"

Adrian looked down at his singed blue robes and blushed, "I don't even know what day it is. It's weird but, since I left here, there has only been now and what needs to happen in this very instant. I've been all over the globe and I've seen some incredible things but I have no sense of time."

"It's Friday night. You have the weekend to rest and recover. I'm afraid that the worst you're facing will only tax your brain, instead of your talents and your bravery."

"To tell the truth, it will be a nice change from all that I've been through. Somehow, class work doesn't seem quite so intimidating anymore."

Sara hugged her son, "I'm just glad that you're safe and we're all together."

"Me too."

They were quiet for a while, before Adrian said, "Zepallo's still out there and I know that, until he is truly defeated, The Balance is not safe."

"There will be time for those battles," smiled his mother. "This is the time for you to grow a bit more as a regular person."

"I wish I'd taken world history, I could write at least three papers on the things that I've learned and the places I've been."

"Maybe next semester," laughed his mother. "The Vatican, the Wailing Wall, and a cave in the Andes?"

"I guess I told those stories at dinner but the one thing that really stuck with me was when I was standing in St. Peter's incredible cathedral and I understood why people come to worship, to talk to their God, to find answers…and I guess I just felt that everyone should be free to pray to whatever God they find in their hearts. It's nobody else's business."

"Did you feel the same way in Jerusalem?"

"Absolutely, I could feel the history, the tension in the energies of that square and I wondered why people can't just let everyone else be who they need to be? That tiny patch of land has been overrun by crusades and wars of one religion fighting another for centuries and that just doesn't make sense to me."

"It hasn't made sense to the grownups since the beginning of time but we keep allowing individuals or small groups to decide what it is we're supposed to believe and every cause needs an enemy, so the most convenient was usually that 'other' religion. Oh, and add that most wars might be started over ideology but the real reason is that to the victors go the plunders. It's about making money, not only what can be stolen from the losers but paying for the troops and their gear, their food and transportation, weapons, and…it goes on and on and someone's making a profit."

"That's just not right."

"Maybe that freedom is part of what you're fighting for?"

"Maybe." Adrian was quiet for a moment, then giggled, "You know, I haven't taken you for a ride on the vectors yet. Would you like to try it?"

His mother blushed, "I'm not sure."

"Oh, come on. It's easy and I know just the place to take you," said Adrian reassuringly. "How about our old house?"

"Okay, that would be lovely, just to see it again. It was home to happy memories."

They stood together and Adrian put his hand on his Mother's shoulder. "Now relax and concentrate on the clearing in the woods behind the house."

A moment later, they were flying along the vectors. The colors streamed past in a dizzying rush and Adrian noticed his Mother's lips curl into an enchanted grin. The connections seemed to be working because there were no bumps or flashes before they touched down beneath the maple trees surrounding their old house by the bay.

"Are you alright?" asked Adrian.

"Oh, that was fun. I can't believe we're here. It seems that no one else is around. The house is dark. Do you think that we could sneak down to sit on the dock for a few minutes?"

"Sure. Let's go."

They walked, hand in hand, down the ramp to the little dock where the Sparrow had been moored for so many years and sat on the edge of the timbers to dangle their feet in the water.

"We had so much fun living here," smiled his mother. "It might not be magical but it's certainly special."

"I loved growing up here and I didn't want to leave," replied Adrian. "But then, I wouldn't have believed the magic of Morgan's Knot or all the weird stuff that's happened since we left."

His mother put her arm around his shoulders and pulled him to her. "I am so proud of you."

They nestled together in the moonlight, startled as a fish leapt from the water and made a small splash. A few bats darted inches above the surface, snatching mosquitoes and moths flying near the dock lights.

Adrian had no time to miss his friends or his normal life. He doubted they would believe any of the things that he had experienced since he saw them last and knew that this was not the moment to go looking for them. He looked down at his ragged blue robes and was sure they would never understand.

As they gazed out at the reflections on the water, a small whirlpool started spinning about fifty feet from the dock. It grew in intensity and a vapor cloud swirled up in the air. They stood to watch the strange disturbance.

A tall, slender figure appeared in the mist, dressed in dark robes, extending long arms out to the sides. A pale face, barely hidden beneath the black cowl, framed cold angry eyes that, again, seemed strangely familiar.

"Zepallo," whispered Adrian, as he stepped in front of his mother.

"We meet again, my young *seer*," smiled the Dark Lord. "I'm afraid that I don't know your name, we haven't been properly introduced."

"I am Adrian. I am a *seer*!" shouted Adrian.

"I'm pleased to meet you…again."

"How did you find us?"

"I was traveling along the vectors and sensed your presence, so I thought we might have a little chat." Zepallo's voice rasped in a loud throaty growl. "I was disappointed that you didn't accept my offer on the mountain. You know it still stands."

"I would never join you because I believe in The Balance and the power of the Light," replied Adrian, slipping hands into the pouches of his robes to find the key, his little penknife, the glasses, the *orb*…and the ring.

He squinted his eyes, sensing the gray aura flickering between waves of light and dark radiating around the Dark Lord. Focusing closer, he saw his own energy combined with his mother's, shimmering brightly like a glowing cocoon. He whispered over his shoulder, "Concentrate on love…on the Light…and the Balance."

The Dark Lord was hovering a few feet above the surface of the water. "You might have caused great havoc and slowed one phase of our program but you'll never defeat me. As you will see, I'll appear again and, this time, no one will impede our progress."

"You'll never win," smiled Adrian. "The Light is stronger than the Dark."

The Dark Lord just laughed. "You haven't introduced me to this lovely lady behind you. Am I to assume this is your mother? How can that be, she is so young?"

"Yes, but I don't introduce those who are special to me to people like you!"

"Be careful, my young *seer*, you don't want to offend me! Besides, in the grand scheme of things, the lineage of those who have ruled the Powers through millennia is a strange, twisted rats' nest of convoluted alliances. We're all related through some ancient sire or dam in the very dawnings of our societies."

"I don't care whether I offend you or not," yelled Adrian. "You represent everything evil in the world."

"Oh, how unkind you are!" smiled the evil one. "Perhaps we should show your mother just how powerful I am!"

Before Adrian could react, Zepallo raised his right hand and a lightning bolt flew from his ring. An image appeared in the mist over the water revealing his mother as a very old and decrepit woman, her eyes desperate and despondent…the pain of a lonely gruesome death.

Sara gasped. Adrian inserted his finger through the ring and pulled it from his pocket. A mighty flash flew across the little bay and the image shattered into a million glittering fragments skipping across the water.

Zepallo smiled, "You see, I can project the future and I can make it into anything that I want it to be. You have no power over me!"

He raised his right hand again and another image appeared of fire raging through the fields on Morgan's Knot, birds and animals stampeding across the island, and the residents crouched in terror on the beaches, helpless against the inferno.

Adrian fired another blast and the images disintegrated. He could feel his mother's panic as her fingers gripped his shoulders.

Zepallo laughed, "Let's see…how about this!" Another flash and a gravestone appeared. It was marked with Adrian's name. His mother gasped, the date of death was today!

The young *seer* squeezed his fingers together and the charge blew the image into tiny shards that traced dark hollows through the haze.

"I could take you today," smiled the Dark Lord, "or tomorrow. Whenever I choose!"

"I'll stand against you right now! You don't have the power to overcome the Light!" screamed Adrian.

"Perhaps I should just turn the lovely Miss Sara into a stone statue!"

Instinctively, Adrian fired a blast at the Dark Lord. A circle of static churned around Zepallo and he gazed at the glowing cloud with an amused smile.

"You see, you do have the darkness within you. You would make a fine apprentice!" smiled the Evil One. "We'll leave that for another day. Your travels through the nodes allowed you to see how weak we humans are. The masses worship their Gods in grand cathedrals and struggle to understand the conflicts in the world around them. The ancients had it right, there is both good and evil in the spiritual realm and, as in a challenging game of chess, pawns must be sacrificed for the greater good. Someday, you'll understand the power of the darkness and appreciate the ancestors who passed on those talents that you are only beginning to acquire."

"The one thing I realized in my travels through the nodes was that every person should have the right to believe what their hearts know to be right and true. You might use weapons or chemicals or germs to kill and destroy but you've no power over their spiritual beliefs."

"Oh, but I do, my young *seer*, as you will see."

"I don't believe you," cried Adrian.

"I would suggest that you pay attention to the news, I have a surprise for you!"

Zepallo's eyes bored into Adrian's mind. The forbidding chill that he felt when he first arrived at the House of the Four Seasons raced up his spine and exploded inside the base of his skull. The Dark Lord's thin lips curled into a knowing smirk as he bowed his head and dissolved. Fading ripples on the water were the only evidence of his presence.

Adrian turned to his mother, pressing his palms to his temples, "I'm sorry you had to witness this confrontation."

His mother wrapped her arms around her son, "I'm glad I was with you. Now I understand what you are fighting. The dark powers are terrifying."

"Yes, they are," sighed Adrian. "But the Light and the Balance are far more powerful than anything he can produce. We will win in the end."

"I pray that you're right," sighed his Mother, staring across the bay. "That man's eyes were, I don't know, strangely familiar or, perhaps, I'm just addled by his use of the Powers for cruelty, domination, and death. I think we should head back to the Island, I don't feel safe here anymore."

They turned to look back at the little house that had been their home for so many years. "This was another lifetime. Things were so normal then."

Adrian smiled, "I know how you feel but we've chosen our path and we must follow it…no matter where it leads."

His mother leaned over and kissed him on the forehead, "Have I mentioned, lately, how much I love you?"

"No, but I love you too!"

"It's time to go," sighed his mother.

Adrian put his hand on her shoulder and smiled up into her beautiful blue eyes, "You are the reason I have to fight Zepallo and his friends. You're everything good in the world and I'm proud that you are my Mother."

With that, they moved into the vectors and flew through the brilliant colors until they landed outside the kitchen door of the House of the Four Seasons.

His Mother hugged him, "It's good to be home."

Later in the evening, Adrian wandered in to flop on Molly's bed to catch the news with the girls. The newscaster on the *messenger* sat in front of a giant map of the world, "Hurricane Francisco, that has threatened Jamaica for the past week, has been down-graded to a tropical storm, as it moves off to the southwest. The island has been spared and residents are cleaning up after a brush with disaster. In other news, representatives from Israel and Palestine sat down together this morning to begin negotiating a settlement…the markets in Japan are on the upswing, after nearly a month of falling stock prices…the Pope appeared in public for the first time in weeks…the communications problems, that have plagued the United States, seem to have been resolved and all systems seem to be functioning normally."

"Weather satellites have detected a volcanic explosion on a small island in the South Atlantic. The destruction seems to have been catastrophic but the island is believed to have been uninhabited."

A short clip showed the Southern Atlantic from hundreds of miles in space. The camera zoomed in on a small, icy island just as a plume of fire exploded out of the sea. Clouds of black smoke erupted and filled the screen. The film cut to a later view of the area where the island had been. There was nothing left but a trail of gray vapor burbling up from the indigo water.

A black and white photograph appeared on the *messenger*, showing the face of the strange gentleman who had arrived in the cove on the Black Diamond only days ago. "In London, Lord Winston Dodd, distant relative of the Royal Family and a power in the international banking community, has gone missing. Although, no ransom note has been received, it is feared that he has been kidnapped…"

The screen switched to a video of a tall, slender figure dressing in flowing white robes, walking slowly near the Temple Mount trailing crowds of the curious and the hopeful. "Finally, tonight, perhaps a message of hope, as a man claiming to be the new Messiah appeared in Jerusalem today. He has been identified by the single name, Palloze, and our reporters caught these few words from him, earlier in the evening, "I bring a message of hope for all the world…"

Adrian stared at the face on the screen and whispered, "Zepallo…"

Characters

Adrian – son of John and Sara, long and lanky with blond hair and
        intense blue eyes

John – Adrian's father, a large man with dark hair and dark eyes, sailor
        and ship designer

Sara – Adrian's mother, blond, blue eyes, housewife, grew up on
        Morgan's Knot

George – Adrian's uncle on Morgan's Knot, tall strong, rough hands,
        salt and pepper hair

Elsie – Adrian's aunt on Morgan's Knot, Sara's sister

Molly and Megan – George & Elsie's twin daughters, blond curly hair,
        blue eyes, a year younger than Adrian

Joshua Keelty– dark eyes, jet black hair – brother of Morgan

Morgan Keelty– tall, long curly brown hair, green eyes, sister of Josh

Ian Sheridan – Kelly's brother, Adrian's second cousin, tall slender

Kelly Sheridan – younger sister of Ian, known for her incredible smile
        brown eyes, blond curls, Adrian's second cousin

Spot and Dusty – dolphins

Professor Ponte – Keeper of the Powers on Morgan's Knot,
        astronomer, teacher - short, fat, bald on top with bushy hair
        growing sides and back, tiny glasses over large eyes and bushy
        eyebrows.

Ester – Ponte's wife - spinsterish, tall, slender, salt and pepper hair,
        highly intelligent, large thick glasses, too small teeth, tight-lipped
        smile

Tic – talking black and white tomcat

Brandy – Keelty's Irish setter

Travis – harbor master

Jasmine – Travis' fishing trawler

Dr. Stevens – doctor on the island

Mrs. Stevens - seamstress

Daphne & Dante – deer, their fowl, Damien
Beggar – small bear
Magnus – large male eagle
Harriet & Harry – hawks
Simian – Jamaican, uncle of Sammy, *seer*
Sammy – nephew of Simian, young Keeper in training

Jofre – Master of the *Others* – giant man with white eyes, father of Alius
Mandor – head of production and security, dark eyes, long straight white hair
Nanchez – Keeper of the dark powers, a giant of a man with white hair, dark eyes
Alius – daughter of Jofre – the Other's *seer*, petite, blond, tough, independent, and beautiful
Aileen – Alius' aunt
Demetre – the Other's harbor master

Blackbeard – monkey on the Island of the Children Raffe – leader of the ghost children
Gabrielle – leader of the Underworld – Mary's husband, long white hair and beard
Dadeus – Keeper of the Powers for the underworld, bald, a child who was left on the island
Mary – Underworld *seer* – Gabrielle's wife
Jim & Morag – Raffe's parents
Soule & Amy – diving instructors
Dee & Slate – dolphins

Additional Characters

Equus – Keeper of the Crystals beneath the Vatican
Captain Max Lee & Second Officer Cameron James & Meteorologist
John Adams – hurricane hunters
Metone & Pegus – whales

Legio Obscurum

The Dark Lord – Zepallo – member of the Council of Ollapez
Sir Winston Dodd – Zepallo's second in command, aristocratic,
      arrogant, ambitious, and subservient to his Master's powers
Reverend Crosby - Whisperer
High-Lord Barrett - Whisperer
Madame Ming – black belt and first-level technician
Captain Foster of the Black Diamond

The Adventure Continues in

Islands of Glass and Steel

Morgan's Knot - A Serial Fantasy
Episode IV

Adrian and Alius struggle to free Raffe, their
friend and fellow *seer*, kidnapped and detained
in Zepallo's secret command center in a
subterranean labyrinth.

Visit www.morgansknot.com

www.ingramcontent.com/pod-product-compliance
Lightning Source LLC
Chambersburg PA
CBHW031058270626
47155CB00026B/1711